W9-CAB-531

EGMONT

We bring stories to life

First published by Egmont USA, 2014
443 Park Avenue South, Suite 806
New York, New York 10016

1 3 5 7 9 8 6 4 2

www.egmontusa.com
www.pennywarner.com
www.CodeBustersClub.com

Interior illustrations by Dave Melvin

LIBRARY OF CONGRESS
CATALOGING-IN-PUBLICATION DATA
Warner, Penny.
The Mummy's Curse / by Penny Warner.
pages cm. — (The Code Busters Club ; case #4)
Summary: A trip to a museum to learn about Ancient Egypt turns into a new case for the Code Busters when they discover that someone may be stealing artifacts and replacing them with cunning forgeries.
ISBN 978-1-60684-459-5 (hardback) — ISBN 978-1-60684-460-1 (eBook)
[1. Cryptography—Fiction. 2. Ciphers—Fiction. 3. Museums—Fiction. 4. Egypt—Antiquities—Fiction. 5. Mystery and detective stories.] I. Title.
PZ7.W2458Mu 2014
[Fic]—dc23
2014003025

Printed in the United States of America

The
CODE BUSTERS

CLUB

CASE #4:

The Mummy's
Curse

Penny Warner

EGMONT
USA
New York

To my Code Busters: Bradley, Luke,
Stephanie, and Lyla

READER

To see keys and solutions to the puzzles inside, go to the Code Buster's Key Book & Solutions on page 169.

To see complete Code Busters Club Rules and Dossiers, and solve more puzzles and mysteries, go to **www.CodeBustersClub.com**

CODE BUSTERS CLUB RULES

Motto
To solve puzzles, codes, and mysteries and
keep the Code Busters Club secret!

Secret Sign
Interlocking index fingers
(American Sign Language sign for "friend")

Secret Password
Day of the week, said backward

Secret Meeting Place
Code Busters Club Clubhouse

Code Busters Club Dossiers

IDENTITY: Quinn Kee

Code Name: "Lock&Key"

Description
Hair: Black, spiky
Eyes: Brown
Other: Sunglasses

Special Skill: Video games, Computers, Guitar

Message Center: Doghouse

Career Plan: CIA cryptographer
or Game designer

Code Specialties: Military code,
Computer codes

IDENTITY: MariaElena—M.E.—Esperanto

Code Name: "Em-me"

Description
Hair: Long, brown
Eyes: Brown
Other: Fab clothes

Special Skill: Handwriting analysis, Fashionista

Message Center: Flower box

Career Plan: FBI handwriting analyst or Veterinarian

Code Specialties: Spanish, I.M., Text messaging

IDENTITY: Luke LaVeau

Code Name: "Kuel-Dude"

Description
Hair: Black, curly
Eyes: Dark brown
Other: Saints cap

Special Skill: Extreme sports, Skateboard, Crosswords

Message Center: Under step

Career Plan: Pro skater, Stuntman, Race car driver

Code Specialties: Word puzzles, Skater slang

IDENTITY: Dakota—Cody—Jones

Code Name: "CodeRed"

Description
Hair: Red, curly
Eyes: Green
Other: Freckles

Special Skill: Languages,
Reading faces and body language

Message Center: Tree knothole

Career Plan: Interpreter for UN or deaf people

Code Specialties: Sign language,
Braille, Morse code, Police codes

CONTENTS*

To crack the chapter title code, check out the CODE BUSTER'S Key Book & Solutions on pp. 171 and 178-179.

Chapter 1

I give up!" Cody said to her mother as she entered the breakfast nook before school Monday morning. Cody bounded into the room dressed in a yellow short-sleeved T-shirt that set off her curly red ponytail. Well-worn jeans and a pair of red Converse Chucks completed her simple outfit. Lately the spring weather had been so sunny, all she'd need was her red hoodie and she'd be set for the short walk to Berkeley Cooperative Middle School.

"What's the matter?" Mrs. Jones asked her

thirteen-year-old daughter, before sipping from a mug of hot, steaming coffee. Already dressed in her uniform, Cody's mother was ready for her job at the Berkeley Police Department. "Did you have trouble figuring out the puzzle Ms. Stadelhofer gave you for homework?"

"No," Cody said and signed, so her deaf four-year-old sister, Tana, would be included in the conversation. "That was pretty easy." She sat down on a stool, filled her bowl with Cheerios, her favorite cereal since she was little, and added milk. "We've been studying ancient Egypt in class, and Ms. Stad gave us these cool decoder cards that have the Egyptian hieroglyphic alphabet, so I knew that was the key." She took a spoonful of cereal.

"What mean h-i-r-o . . . ?" Tana tried to finger-spell the word.

Code Buster's Key and Solution found on pp. 171, 173.

Cody slowly respelled the word using the American Sign Language manual alphabet, then

2

signed, "Hieroglyphs are like words and stories written in pictures."

She turned to her mother. "We're going to the Rosicrucian Egyptian Museum in San Jose on Friday to see some hieroglyphs and ancient artifacts, and even a mummy." Cody had never seen a mummy before, except in movies, and *they* always looked fake. She wondered if she'd be creeped out by a real one.

"So what's the problem?" her mother asked.

"I'm not sure what Ms. Stad's word means." Cody took out the assignment from her backpack and showed it to her mom. Written underneath the hiero-glyphic symbols was Cody's English translation.

Code Buster's Key and Solution found on pp. 172, 173.

Cody's mom looked at the decoded word her daughter had written. "Did you look it up?"

"The dictionary says it means 'concealed writ-ing'—kind of like a hidden message. But that's all I know."

"Hmm," her mom murmured. "It sounds like

3

Ms. Stadelhofer has another mysterious puzzle for you to solve."

"Seriously! I hope there are a bunch of hidden messages at the museum. Ms. Stad said the place is full of mysteries. She said to make sure we study our latest spelling words, because they'll be part of our assignment. I have a feeling she's making up some puzzles for us, too."

"Sounds fun. Do you want me to quiz you?" Cody's mother asked.

"Sure." Cody handed the word list to her mother. Cody was a good speller. She'd taught herself tricks for remembering difficult words and almost always got 100 percent on her tests. But this time she might not do as well because these new words were so different. They were the names of Egyptian gods and goddesses.

As her mother read off each spelling word, Cody wrote it down on a piece of paper. Most of the names weren't too hard—*Amun, Anubis, Bastet, Horus, Isis, Osiris, Sekhmet, Sobek*. She could sound them out. But *Maat* was tricky—two *a*'s instead of two *t*'s

4

like Matt the Brat. And *Thoth* was pronounced *toth*, so she had to remember to add the silent *h*.

"How'd I do?" she asked her mother after she'd corrected the test.

"Perfect, as usual," her mom said. "Do you have to know why all the gods and goddesses were worshipped? They each had their specific purposes."

"Yep, I memorized them, and we picked our favorites as our Egyptian Code Buster names," Cody replied. "Let's see. Amun was the god of air and invisibility. That's the one I chose, because I'd love to be invisible sometimes and just watch people. Anubis was the god of death. Bastet was the cat goddess. M.E. chose that one because she loves animals. Horus was the god of war and the sky. Isis was the goddess of magic. That's Quinn's favorite, since he's been learning magic tricks. Maat was the goddess of truth and justice. Osiris was the god of the underworld and afterlife. Sekhmet was the goddess of lions and power. That's Luke's Egyptian code name, because he's strong. Then there's Sobek . . . Sobek . . . um . . ." Cody shook her head.

"I think he's the god of crocodiles," Mrs. Jones said.

"Right! Crocodiles," Cody said. "And the last one is Thoth, the god of wisdom. I just have to remember Sobek. Then I'll know them all!"

"Good morning, students," Ms. Stadelhofer said to her class of sixth graders after the students were settled in their seats. "As we discussed on Friday, the study of ancient Egypt has been steeped in mystery for centuries. Scholars tried to decode the hieroglyphs over the years, but it wasn't until the Rosetta Stone was discovered in 1799 that they even had a clue how to crack the code. And it still took another twenty years for scholars to decipher all the writings on the stone."

A student named Bradley raised his hand. "Twenty years? That's a long time. It only took me about twenty seconds to decode the message you gave us for homework."

"Excellent," Ms. Stad said. "How about the rest of you?"

Several students raised their hands, including

Cody. She loved how Ms. Stad always made her lessons fun. She often created puzzles for them to solve and made up games to help them learn. She even wore creative outfits, like college T-shirts, historical costumes, and arty jackets. Today she was dressed in safari pants and a khaki top with the words YOU CAN'T SCARE ME—I TEACH SIXTH GRADE! Around her neck she'd draped a long knitted scarf decorated with Egyptian characters. All she needed was a pith helmet to complete the outfit and she'd be ready for an archaeological dig.

The homework assignment had been fun, too. Cody thought it would be cool to send coded messages in hieroglyphs to her Code Busters Club friends. She and MariaElena—M.E.—Esperanto, Quinn Kee, and Luke LaVeau were always looking for new codes to crack. And hieroglyphs were awesome because they looked like pictures.

Cody pulled out her homework and read over her answers to make sure they were correct.

STEGANOGRAPHY

One of the pictographs—the letter *s*—looked like an upside-down hook. The *t* reminded her of a mountain. The *e* was represented by an arm. The *g* looked like a badge. And the letter *a* was some kind of bird. All the rest of the letters resembled something familiar—a zigzag for *n*, a lamp for *o*, a flying saucer for *r*, a shelf for *p*, a square curling in on itself for *h*, two feathers for *y*. The associations made them easier to remember.

"We can now understand the Egyptian alphabet," said Ms. Stad, "primarily because a soldier named Pierre-François Bouchard found a stone in Rosetta, Egypt. That's why it's called the Rosetta Stone. Years later, a teenager named Jean-François Champollion began decoding the stone. It took him fourteen years! Can you imagine working on a puzzle that long?"

The students shook their heads. Cody was impressed.

Ms. Stad smiled. "The young man finally figured out that hieroglyphs were not really pictures but signs for sounds, just like we use in English. For example, the image of the upside-down hook is the sound for *s*. So, who can tell us what the homework message says?" asked Ms. Stad.

Most of the students raised their hands. Ms. Stad called on Cody.

"Steganography," Cody said, hoping she pronounced it correctly.

"Right. Do you know what that means?" Ms. Stad asked her.

"I looked it up. It means 'the practice of concealed writing' or 'creating hidden messages.'"

"Exactly," Ms. Stad exclaimed. "*Stegano* comes from the Greek word for 'covered' or 'hidden,' and *graphia* or *graphy* is Latin for 'writing.'" She glanced around at the students. "How many of you got it right?"

Most of the students put their hands up again. Cody noticed that Matt the Brat wasn't one of them. She figured he probably didn't even do the assignment—as usual. How was he ever going to make it to seventh grade?

"Good job, students!" Ms. Stad smiled. "As Cody said, *steganography* means 'the art of hiding secret messages in plain sight.' When you look at Egyptian drawings, they appear to be random pictures—at first. But if you study them, you'll find they have hidden meanings. Does anyone know other ways of hiding a message in plain sight?"

M.E., Cody's friend who sat in the back of the classroom, raised her hand. "You could write a message on an envelope and cover it with a postage stamp," she said, "and then steam off the stamp to read the message." The Code Busters were very familiar with that method of sending hidden messages. They often mailed each other notes in code, with the key hidden under a stamp on the envelope.

"Yes, M.E., that was a popular method for spies who wanted to send top secret information over long distances during wartime. Does anyone else know how to hide a message?"

Matt the Brat blurted out, "You could shave your head and write a secret message with a marker and then grow your hair back and it would be hidden."

"True, Matthew," Ms. Stad said. "Soldiers often did that. But they wouldn't just write a secret message on the person's head. They *tattooed* it."

"No way!" Matt said, rubbing his head. "That would hurt!"

Ms. Stad smiled patiently. "There are lots of ways to hide messages. I could even be hiding one in the scarf I'm wearing today. While you're looking at the Egyptian symbols on the scarf, the real message could be hidden by tying knots into the strands of yarn using Morse code. Spies used to knit the knotted yarn into a sweater or scarf, and the person who received the item simply unraveled it to decode the knotted message."

Awesome, Cody thought. She would have to try that. As soon as she learned to knit. She glanced back at M.E. and finger-spelled:

Code Buster's Key and Solution found on pp. 171, 173.

"Now, I've got a surprise for you, class," Ms. Stad announced, interrupting M.E.'s message back to Cody.

The buzzing students quieted down and waited for their teacher's announcement.

"We have a special guest. I've invited the curator from the Rosicrucian Egyptian Museum to come and tell you all about puzzles, codes, and messages that are hidden in art—another form of steganography."

Ms. Stad turned to a woman who had just entered the classroom. She was tall and thin, with white-blonde hair twisted up at the back, vivid green eyes thickly outlined in black, and bright red lipstick. She wore a black turtleneck, black slacks, and black high-heeled shoes, but what caught Cody's attention was the pendant she wore around her neck. It was a large golden "eye," about the size of an Oreo cookie, heavily outlined in black, much like the woman's eyes. Her hands were covered with large gold rings, one in the shape of an eye that nearly matched the one on her necklace.

Cody was intrigued by the woman's exotic looks, clothes, and jewelry—especially the eye that hung from her neck. The woman played with her necklace nervously as she faced the class. Cody wondered if she wasn't used to speaking to school students.

"Everyone, this is Ms. Mirabel Cassatt. Please welcome our special guest!"

The students greeted her in unison.

"Hello, students." Ms. Cassatt stepped forward on her tall, spiked heels and spoke softly as she continued to fuss with her pendant.

Ms. Stad grinned at the class. "Do any of you know what a museum curator does?"

No one answered.

"Well," Ms. Stad began, "a curator is generally in charge of the museum. She obtains art and antiquities, authenticates them to make sure they're real, sets up the exhibits, and plans educational programs for students and the public."

Ms. Cassatt nodded. "That's right. Plus, there's a lot of paperwork," she added.

"Does anyone know what we call the object on Ms. Cassatt's necklace?"

"A mutant cyclops?" Matt the Brat called out. The class laughed.

"No," Ms. Stad said, after giving Matt a stern look. "Anyone else?"

A girl named Iman raised her hand. "It looks like an eye."

"That's right," Ms. Cassatt said. "It's a replica of an amulet called the Eye of Horus. The real ones were considered to be magic charms in ancient Egypt and symbolized the ability to see wisdom and truthfulness. The All-Seeing Eye was often buried with its owner to protect him or her in the afterlife. Mine is similar to one of the many artifacts you'll see when you come to the Egyptian Museum later this week."

"Is that really from ancient Egypt?" Matt blurted out.

Ms. Cassatt clutched the pendant. "No, as I said, this is a replica. The real ones are in museums. I'd have to have an armed guard with me if this one was authentic, or someone might steal it."

"Is it worth a lot of money?" Matt asked, ignoring Ms. Stad's glare.

Ms. Cassatt laughed. "Not this one. But the ones in the museum are priceless."

Cody wondered whether she would get to see

some really valuable artifacts when they visited the museum. And whether the artifacts would be under armed guard to protect them from thieves, like Matt the Brat. Last year, he'd stolen a kid's bike and had been suspended from school for a whole week.

"Today, class, Ms. Cassatt is going to show you another reproduction—a famous painting," Ms. Stad continued. "Look at it carefully. It contains a secret message."

Ms. Stad pressed a button on her projector remote, and the large image of a painting appeared on the whiteboard. Cody recognized the work of art immediately. The painting was one of her favorites because of the woman's mysterious smile.

"Does anyone know what this is?"

Several hands shot up, including Cody's. Ms. Stad called on Miranda, who sat in the front row. Miranda was a good artist herself. Cody had seen her anime drawings in class and wished she were as talented. The best Cody could do was draw regular old stick figures.

"That's the *Mona Lisa* by Leonardo da Vinci," Miranda answered. "I saw it in person when my family went to the Louvre during our vacation in Paris last year."

"Yeah?" said Matt the Brat. "Well, I saw it in a cartoon, and when she smiled, she didn't have any teeth." He laughed loudly at his own joke.

Ms. Stad eyed him. "Matthew, please raise your hand if you have something to say." He quieted down under her glare.

"You're right, Miranda," Ms. Cassatt said. "This work is known as the *Mona Lisa* and is probably the most famous painting in the world. There's a lot of mystery about it. Who is the woman? And why is she smiling like that?"

Matt turned in his seat and whispered to Cody, "She has to fart!" Cody rolled her eyes.

Ms. Cassatt continued unaware of Matt's latest interruption. "Did you know that the *Mona Lisa* was stolen about a hundred years ago from the Louvre? Someone who worked at the museum hid in a broom closet until after the exhibits closed, then walked out with the painting under his coat! But when he tried to sell it, he was caught and sent to jail. Now it's kept under bulletproof glass."

"Wow," said a couple of kids.

"Is it at your Egyptian Museum?" Avery asked.

"No, we only collect things from ancient Egypt," Ms. Cassatt said.

Avery raised her hand again. "Have you ever had anything stolen from *your* museum?"

Ms. Cassatt frowned. "I certainly hope not. About a year ago, we hired a forgery expert named Malik Jordan, so I doubt we'll have any problems like that, since security is strong."

There were a few more oohs and aahs from the class. Then Ms. Cassatt said, "Now, back to the painting. I have a puzzle for you. Do any of you notice anything strange about Mona Lisa's eyes?"

The students shook their heads. Cody stared at the dark, deep-set eyes in the reproduction but didn't notice anything unusual.

Ms. Stad pushed a button on her device. An enlargement of one eye appeared on the whiteboard.

Ms. Cassatt pointed to the pupil, the darkest part of the eye. "This is Mona Lisa's right eye, close-up. Experts believe there's a message hidden in the eyes of the portrait. But you can only see it when the eyes are enlarged. Look closely. See if you can find anything in this eye."

A few seconds later, Cody raised her hand. "Are they letters?"

"Yes," Ms. Cassatt said. "Can you tell me which ones?"

"It looks like an *L* and a *V*."

"Right again," Ms. Cassatt said. "Now, do any of you know why Leonardo da Vinci might have painted those letters inside the pupil of Mona Lisa's right eye?"

To Cody it was obvious. "Because they're his initials?"

"Very good," Ms. Cassatt said.

"Are there initials in the other eye?" a student named Ryan asked.

Another enlarged photograph of an eye appeared on the whiteboard. To Cody, it looked very similar to the first one, but this time, the letters weren't as clear.

"Yes," Ms. Cassatt said, "but no one has ever figured out what they are or what they mean. Does anyone here think they know?"

Hands went up. "The letters *C* and *E*?" Ryan offered.

Ms. Cassatt shook her head.

"The letter *B*," guessed a boy named Ty.

"See, that's the problem," said Ms. Cassatt. "We don't know, because the portrait is old and the paint has deteriorated over time. It remains a mystery."

Cody wondered if she and the Code Busters could solve the puzzle of Mona Lisa's left eye. But if experts had been trying for years, it was very unlikely.

Ms. Cassatt showed several more paintings and artifacts and explained the symbols in them.

"If you look around carefully, you can see alphabet letters in everyday objects, and you can use them to send hidden messages," Ms. Cassatt said. "For example, a chair can look like the letter *h*, a pole can look like an *i*, and so on." She showed the students drawings of a chair, a pole, two musical notes, a shelf, and a tunnel entrance. "Each one could be viewed as a letter if you looked at them just the right way. What do these letters spell out?" she asked the class.

It took a few seconds before the letters jumped out of the drawings. Once Cody saw them, she wondered why it had taken her so long. Before she could raise her hand, M.E. beat her to it and gave the answer.

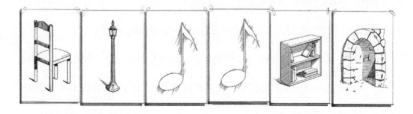

Code Buster's Solution found on p. 173.

"Right," Ms. Cassatt said. She outlined the letters in each drawing with an electronic pointer so that the rest of the students could *see* the message. "Sometimes you have to look at something for a while to really see it!"

Clever, Cody thought. She glanced around the room and began to notice letters everywhere. She saw the letter *C* in the stand that held the world globe, an *O* in the clock on the wall, a *D* in the musical note on the whiteboard, and an *E* in the small bookshelf. Using her cell phone camera, she snapped a picture of each one so she could create a coded message for the Code Busters later.

Code Buster's Solution found on p. 173.

"And now, students," Ms. Stad said, "I'd like you all to create your own picture. Feel free to use the computer. Just remember to include a hidden message inside. Once you're all finished, we'll line them up along the whiteboard and try to decipher what they mean."

Cody looked back at M.E. and smiled. This was going to be awesome!

Chapter 2

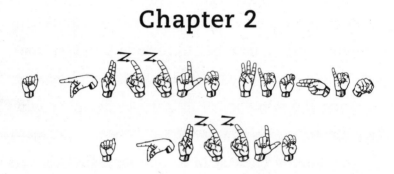

Cody began her picture by drawing seven stick figures, each standing in different positions. Next, she added a prop to each one, to make the figures look as if they were doing something. In the first figure's hand, she drew a stop sign. In the second, she added cheerleader pom-poms. She made the third one look like it was walking a couple of dogs attached to leashes. For the fourth one, she wove a long string through both its hands, leading to a flying kite. The next figure looked as if it were reaching for something. The one after that held a long stick with two pails balanced at each end. And the last one appeared to be walking on a balance beam.

Satisfied with her simple drawing—and the coded semaphore message it contained—she wrote a cryptic title for the picture:

artistic –talented –inspired images

She was careful to write all the letters in lower-case, and made sure the dashes were attached to the beginnings of the words *talented* and *inspired*. She deliberately left off the period at the end of the sentence, to avoid confusion.

When she was finished, she double-checked her work to make sure the message was accurate. She was pretty sure that only one person in the class would be able to decipher the hidden message in her artwork: M.E. Her friend was as good at cracking codes as Cody was. That's why they had joined Quinn and Luke to form the Code Busters Club.

"All right, class," Ms. Stad announced. "You've had plenty of time to design a picture with an embedded message. Bring your pictures up to the front, one row at a time, and tape them to the whiteboard. Then we'll see if we can find the hidden message in each picture."

In an orderly fashion, the students brought their artwork to the board. After everyone had returned to their seats, Ms. Stad pointed to the first picture and asked who had made it. M.E. raised her hand. Cody knew her friend's hidden message would be a challenging one to solve.

At first glance, it looked to Cody like a bunch of alphabet letters in the shape of a tree.

```
           c
          lay
         lines
        redyarn
       artcolors
      hueglueblue
     purpleribbons
    pinkgreenlights
   ayellowpaintbrush
  artcanvasdesigndark
         ime
         see
```

Code Buster's Solution found on p. 173.

Then she began to see words within the tree—
clay, lines, red yarn. She quickly realized that most
of the words were related to art in some way. *Cool!*
Cody thought.

"Does anyone know what the hidden message
is?" Ms. Stad asked after a few minutes.

Hands shot into the air, but Cody hung back to
give the others a chance to answer. Ms. Stad called

on several students, who announced the words they saw in the letter tree. But Cody had a feeling there was more to it than just art-related words. M.E. must have hidden something else.

"Did they figure out your message, MariaElena?" Ms. Stad asked, calling the girl by her full name.

"Only part of it," M.E. replied with a grin. "There's more."

I knew it! Cody thought. She studied the letters and wondered why M.E. had arranged them in that particular design. Why a tree and not a spiral or a box? And although the words were related to art, they still seemed kind of random. Red yarn? Art colors? Hue glue blue? Why didn't M.E. just write a continuing sentence using the tree shape?

Because, Cody realized suddenly, M.E. had spelled out a message that read *down,* not across!

Cody jotted down the message and raised her hand before anyone else.

"Cody?" Ms. Stad said. "Do you know the answer?"

Cody stood and approached the picture. "The message is actually written down the middle of the tree letters." She ran a finger down the letters in the center as she said the words aloud.

The class voiced a collective "Ahh!" as they finally recognized M.E.'s concealed message. Cody turned to her friend at the back and grinned. M.E. gave her a thumbs-up.

"Good job, Cody!" Ms. Stad said, looking pleased as Cody returned to her seat. "All right, class. Are you ready for the next one?" Cody's teacher indicated a drawing that looked like a maze.

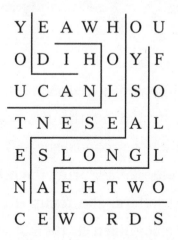

Code Buster's Solution found on p. 174.

This is an easy one, Cody thought. All she had to do was follow the letters to make a word, then follow the words to make a sentence. Moments later she raised her hand, along with M.E. and several other students. Ms. Stad called on Lauren, who went to the board and pointed out the hidden message as she read it aloud.

"Excellent, Lauren," Ms. Stad said. She pointed to the next picture, composed of three drawings. To Cody, it looked like a bunch of fancy squiggles.

Code Buster's Solution found on p. 174.

Cody concentrated on the first drawing. After staring at it for a few seconds, she saw the shape of a letter begin to emerge. Figuring the other two drawings were also letters, she focused on the second one until she recognized it, then studied the third one. Together the three letters formed a word! *Cool,* Cody thought. She liked how the student had made each hidden letter look like a work of art.

"Whose picture is this?" Ms. Stad asked the class.

To Cody's surprise, Matt raised his hand. Wow. She never knew he had such talent. Most of his artwork was monsters and dragons.

"Nice job, Matthew," Ms. Stad said.

The picture puzzle activity continued through the rest of the student drawings. Cody was able to decipher all of them, although a couple were harder to crack than others. Finally, Ms. Stad came to Cody's picture, which was next to last.

artistic –talented –inspired images

"Who drew that one?" Matt the Brat said loudly. "It's just a bunch of stick figures. There's no hidden message. It says right above: 'artistic, talented, inspired images.' That's lame."

Ms. Stad glared at Matt, who sat in front of Cody. "Matthew, if you speak without raising your hand one more time, you're going to Mr. Grant's office. Do you understand?"

Matt slunk down in his chair, red-faced, and stared at his desktop. Ms. Stad often had to send Matt to the principal's office for misbehaving in class. Cody wondered if Mr. Grunt—er, Grant—was sick of seeing him every week.

"Now," Ms. Stad continued, "does anyone see a hidden message in this picture?"

A few hands went up. Cody listened to some of the wild guesses about her drawing.

"Are the stick figures supposed to be shaped like letters?" Annika asked.

"Do the words at the top have words inside them?" asked Liam.

"Is the message written in invisible ink?" said Thomas in the front row.

"It seems to be very complex," Ms. Stad said, staring at the picture. She looked out at her students. "Whose picture is this?"

Cody raised her hand.

"Cody, are any of those answers correct?"

Ms. Stad asked.

"Nope," she said, feeling proud that no one had cracked the code yet.

"Could you give us a hint?" Ms. Stad suggested.

"Okay, well, the stick figures don't form letters, but they do stand for letters. . . ."

"They're semaphores!" announced a boy named Connor after Ms. Stad called on him. "They're supposed to be holding flags, but if you look at the position of their arms, you can figure out what each letter is. The first one is *b*—"

"Don't tell!" Ms. Stad said. "Let the rest of the students try to decode the letters by themselves. Everyone, use your semaphore decoder card to find the answer."

The students pulled out their decoder cards from their desks. As part of their language unit, Ms. Stadelhofer had made decoder cards for the students for each new code they were learning. The kids thumbed through their packs until they found the one with semaphores. Moments later, most of the students had translated the stick figure message.

Ms. Stad called on Spencer, Connor's twin brother, who gave the answer.

"But I still don't know what it's supposed to mean," Spencer said, frowning.

"There's more to it," Cody said to the class. "You're supposed to look at the title of the picture, too."

The students continued to study Cody's picture, but no one said anything more.

"How about another hint?" Ms. Stad said.

"Okay, um . . . remember what Ms. Stad taught us during handwriting: Don't forget to dot your *i*'s and cross your *t*'s."

After a few minutes, one hand went up.

"MariaElena?" Ms. Stad said. "Do you know the answer?"

She nodded, grinning. "The title is actually written in *hidden* Morse code."

"Nuh-uh," said Matt the Brat, raising his hand. "There's no dots or dashes."

M.E. stood up and moved to the front of the room. She pointed to the first word, *artistic,* then said, "Do you see any dots or dashes in that word?"

"Ooh!" said several class members, as they realized what she meant.

Connor raised his hand. "The *t*'s and *i*'s are supposed to be dashes and dots! The code hidden in the word *artistic* is actually *t i t i*—dash, dot, dash, dot. That's the letter *c* in Morse code!"

"Very good, Connor!" Ms. Stad wrote the dots, dashes, and letters on the board above the picture as the students called them out.

t i t i -.-. t t t - - - t i i -.. i .

Using their Morse code decoder cards, the students quickly deciphered the hidden message.

Code Buster's Key and Solution found on pp. 170 and 171, 174.

"Nice work, Cody!" Ms. Stad said. "You hid the message well, yet it was still right in front of our eyes. I love the way you used pictures and words to hide two different messages. That's a perfect example of steganography."

Cody felt her face flush hot. She was glad her teacher liked her work, but she was embarrassed to receive such praise in front of everyone. She returned to her seat and sat down, hoping the other students would stop looking at her.

"All right, class," Ms. Stad said, drawing attention away from Cody. "There's one last picture. Does anyone know what the concealed message is here?" She pointed to the image.

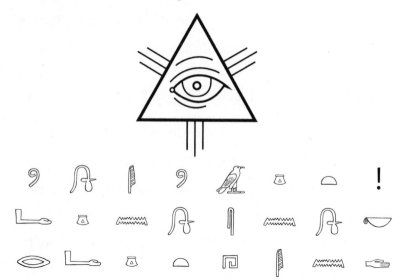

The students grew silent as they gazed at the picture of a triangle with an eye in the middle. To Cody, the drawing sort of looked Egyptian, reminding her of the pendant Ms. Cassatt wore around her neck, but she had no idea what it was supposed to mean.

It didn't appear to have any letters or symbols, other than an eye and a triangle. Was there really a message hidden in the picture? She worked on translating the Egyptian hieroglyphs underneath, but the letters formed nonsensical words.

For the first time in a long while, Cody was completely stumped.

Chapter 3

Ms. Stad waited a few more seconds to see if anyone could decipher the last picture. When no one raised a hand, she announced, "It seems as though we have a real mystery here. I think we need a clue. Who did the picture?"

She glanced around the room, searching for a raised hand. No response. "Anyone?" Frowning, she turned back to the last picture on the board. "That's very strange. Well, since we haven't figured out the hidden message, I'll make that your assignment for

Friday. If you can decipher the meaning behind the image, you'll get extra credit. Perhaps then we'll find out who created it!"

While most of the students, including M.E., copied the drawing on paper, Cody and a few others got out their cell phones and snapped pictures of the mysterious eye-in-a-triangle design. Cody planned to take the snapshot to the Code Busters Clubhouse after school and share it with Luke and Quinn. This mysterious message obviously required all four of their code-busting brains.

When the three o'clock bell rang, Cody and M.E. met outside of class and headed for their clubhouse. It was hidden in the eucalyptus forest nearby.

"Figure out the message yet?" M.E. asked as they trudged up the densely forested hill.

"No, you?" Cody asked, pulling out her phone to look at the picture. "I thought maybe it was a rebus—one of those messages written mostly in pictures. Like, the eye could stand for the letter *i*. But what would the triangle stand for?"

M.E. shrugged. "Maybe we can do a Google

search for the different meanings of the word *triangle* when we get to the clubhouse."

Cody nodded. She took one last look at the puzzling picture, then returned her phone to her pocket for the rest of the short climb. "Come on. I'm sure the guys are already waiting for us. They always beat us there."

"That's because they run here right after they get out of Mr. Pike's class," M.E. said. "I'm too tired after school to run anywhere."

Several minutes later, they arrived at the small shack the Code Busters had made out of old wooden billboard panels. Over the top they'd spread a camouflage parachute, which formed the roof and disguised the rest of the clubhouse.

Cody gave the secret knock, tapping out her initials in Morse code, followed by M.E.

$$- \cdot \cdot \quad \cdot - - - \quad - - \quad \cdot$$

Code Buster's Key and Solution found on pp. 170, 174.

Then she said that day's password: "Yadnom."

Code Buster's Solution found on p. 174.

Cody heard scuffling behind the door. Finally, Quinn opened it, letting Cody and M.E. inside before replacing the board that kept out snoops, mountain lions, and Matt the Brat. The girls unloaded their backpacks and joined Luke and Quinn on the newly carpeted floor. They'd found the large remnant behind the school and had carried it up the hill to place over the cold sheet-metal floor.

The boys appeared to have been working on some kind of picture puzzle. Quinn held his cell phone over a sheet that featured both sides of a dollar bill.

"What are you guys doing?" M.E. asked, glancing at the paper that lay in front of them.

"Homework," Luke said. "We're studying steganography. Our teacher wants us to find all the hidden symbols on a dollar bill. Quinn's using the magnifying glass app on his phone."

"We're studying steganography, too," Cody said. "But Ms. Stad gave us a different drawing to figure out—not a dollar bill. We're hoping you can help us crack it."

"Sure, after you help us with ours." Quinn pulled out a real dollar from his pocket and held it up to the light coming in through the thin fabric roof.

"What are you doing?" M.E. asked.

"Just checking to see if this has a watermark. It's one of those invisible images you can only see when you hold paper up to the light. That way, you can tell if it's counterfeit." He stared at the bill. "This one doesn't have a watermark. It doesn't even have a security thread."

"What's a security thread?" M.E. asked.

Quinn pulled another bill out of his pocket, this

time a five. He held it up to the light. "There's the watermark," he said, pointing to a faint circle that had been pressed into the bill. "See that line down the side? That's the security thread."

"Cool!" M.E. said, holding up the bill and examining it. "I never knew that was in there!"

Quinn nodded. "My dad showed me. I guess it's only in bills that are worth more than a dollar, because dollar bills don't have them."

"But we did find some hidden stuff on the one-dollar bill," Luke said. "Like this hidden spider." He pointed to a tiny dot near the number *1* in the upper right corner of the illustration.

"I think it looks like an owl," Quinn said. "And the number *thirteen* is hidden all over the place. See? The eagle on the back is holding thirteen arrows. The branch in its right foot has thirteen leaves. The shield has thirteen stripes, and there are thirteen stars over the eagle's head. Even the pyramid has thirteen steps."

"Why are there so many thirteens?" M.E. asked. "Isn't that supposed to be an unlucky number?"

Quinn shook his head. "Our teacher said it represents the original thirteen colonies."

"Wait a minute!" Cody said, raising her head. She'd been studying the back of the one-dollar bill intensely. "Check out the pyramid. There's an eye at the top, inside a triangle! Just like the one in that picture, M.E.!"

She tapped the photo icon on her phone to retrieve the snapshot she'd taken of the mysterious drawing. "M.E., get the picture you drew of that triangle/eye." While M.E. pulled out her drawing, Cody showed the boys the photo of the puzzling artwork. It still had her stumped.

"You're right," Luke said. "It does look like the same symbol as the one on the dollar bill. What do you think it means?"

"That's a good question," Cody said. She clicked a search engine icon on her phone, then typed in the words *triangle eye*. After reading the information, she looked up at the other Code Busters. "It's Egyptian!"

"That's weird," M.E. said. "We're studying

Egyptian stuff right now. What else does it say?"

"It says here the symbol is called the All-Seeing Eye of Providence or the Eye of Horus. We learned about that in class. It's like a lucky charm that's supposed to watch over everyone."

"That doesn't tell us much," Luke said.

"Look up 'Eye of Horus,'" Quinn said to Cody. "Maybe that will give us more information than what our teachers told us."

Cody typed in the words, then read from the entry. "It says, in ancient Egypt, the Eye of Horus was a symbol of protection, power, and good health. They used to make amulets—jewelry—in the shape of the Eye, and bury them with people to protect them in the afterlife and ward off evil spirits."

"Wow," M.E. said. "Kinda creepy."

Cody read on. "It says Horus was a sky god who looked like a falcon and that the eye is supposed to look like a falcon's eye. When Horus got in a fight with another god, his eye got poked out, so he gave it to his dad to save his life."

"Weird," Luke said.

"The Eye of Horus was even used to measure fractions," Cody added.

"Yeah, I remember Ms. Stad told us that Horus was some kind of sky god," M.E. said.

"His right eye represented the sun god, Ra," Cody continued.

"And the other eye represented the moon," Luke added.

"Hmm," M.E. said. "So the eyes have hidden meanings, sort of like the *Mona Lisa*'s eyes."

"What are you guys talking about?" Luke asked, frowning.

Cody explained what they had learned about the initials hidden in the da Vinci painting.

"But what does that have to do with the Eye of Horus? And the stuff on a dollar bill? I still don't get it," Luke said, looking back and forth between M.E.'s drawing of the Eye and the picture on the dollar bill.

"You think it's some kind of code?" Quinn asked Cody.

"It has to be," Cody said. "We just have to figure out what it means. Ms. Stad said we get extra credit

44

if we can solve it."

Cody checked the Internet dictionary on her phone for a definition of the word *triangle*. "It says here, 'A triangle is a plane figure formed by connecting three points not in a straight line by straight line segments.'" *That's not helpful,* Cody thought. She searched and found several more definitions, all containing the word *three*. Then she found a link to the phrase *third eye*.

She felt a tingle down her back and clicked the link.

Cody's eyes lit up. "Guys, listen to this. A triangle with an eye in it can mean 'third eye.'"

"So what's a third eye?" M.E. asked.

"It means seeing something more than what's right in front of you," Cody replied.

"Like a ghost?" Luke said, grinning and wiggling his fingers.

Cody smiled. "Very funny. Seriously, if you think about it, art is also about seeing more than what's right in front of you. It's seeing the real meaning of a picture or sculpture or whatever."

"Sort of like a hidden message?" Quinn suggested.

M.E. grinned. "Like steganography!"

By Friday, the day of the field trip to the museum, Cody was still puzzling over the mysterious picture of the triangle/eye. Did it really represent a third eye? Or was she way off track and letting her imagination run away with her?

She and M.E. had talked about the picture puzzle the whole way to school. By the time they reached the school grounds, Cody couldn't wait to find out what the puzzle actually meant and hoped Ms. Stad would tell them right away. Maybe it had something to do with their field trip.

Ms. Stad greeted the girls at the waiting bus and checked their names off her list as they got on. Cody and M.E. found seats at the back of the bus, in front of Luke and Quinn.

Cody turned around to look at the boys. "Did you guys figure out the puzzle yet?"

"Nope," Quinn answered.

Luke shook his head. "You?"

Before she could answer, Ms. Stad called for everyone's attention. Maybe now she'd reveal the secret.

"All right, students! Quiet down, please, and take your seats. We're about to leave, and I want everyone to be safe. Matthew! Sit down!"

Cody rolled her eyes at Matt the Brat, who was standing up and sticking his head out the window. She was surprised he'd been allowed to go on the trip, since he'd been to the principal's office twice this week. She just hoped he didn't ruin the trip for everyone.

Cody loved going to museums with her dad. Since her parents were divorced, her dad always came up with something fun to do on their weekends together. She'd seen an entomology exhibit (bugs), a paleontology exhibit (dinosaurs), and a vertebrate exhibit (snakes), but her favorite one had been called "Bodies." The exhibit was made of displays showing the insides of real human bodies—the skeletal, muscular, nervous, respiratory, digestive, and circulatory systems. Somehow they'd managed to preserve the bodies, sort of like mummies. The bodies were weird, creepy, and awesome, all at the same time. Cody wondered if the mummies at the Egyptian Museum would be as creepy and cool.

The Code Busters spent the hour's drive creating hieroglyphic codes for each other to decipher. Cody's message read:

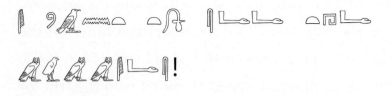

M.E. wrote:

Quinn wrote:

And Luke wrote:

Code Buster's Key and Solutions found on pp. 172, 174.

Before they knew it, the bus had pulled up to the museum parking lot. Ms. Stad and Mr. Pike reviewed the rules about conduct and safety, and offered some information on the museum, then let the students off the bus.

"Students, as you know, the museum houses over four thousand artifacts," Mr. Pike said. "There are four major rooms to explore—the Daily Life room, the Burial Practices room, the Gods and Religion room, and the Kings and Pharaohs room. And there's even a dark, underground tunnel with twists and turns and hidden alcoves that simulates an ancient Egyptian tomb, with a real mummy at the end. So be warned."

The students buzzed. Cody knew Quinn and

Luke would be excited to see a real mummy, but she also knew M.E. wanted nothing to do with what she called "dried-up dead people." M.E. was afraid of everything, from mummies to monsters to mutant zombies. As for Cody, she was curious, but wasn't sure how she'd react when she actually saw a mummy.

A student from Cody's class, named Jack, raised his hand. "When are we going to find out what the picture means?"

Good question, Cody thought.

Ms. Stad eyed the group mysteriously. "Soon, I hope. Now, gather your backpacks, stay with your buddies, and we'll meet just inside the lobby."

Cody tried to visualize what a mummy looked like as she and M.E. followed their paired classmates past a labyrinth garden, a water fountain flanked by two human-headed lions, and an adobe building painted with Egyptian hieroglyphs. Would it look like a person? A body wrapped in a white sheet? A "dried-up dead person," as M.E. said?

And how did they even make a mummy, anyway?

The students filed into the building in pairs under the steely eyes of two security guards at the door. Cody read their name tags—SIMON WOOD and DEBORAH WEINSTEIN—and wondered if they ever had any problems at the museum with people stealing stuff. Or were they there just to let visitors know they were being watched? The man eyed Cody as she passed by, a frown on his face, as if he suspected she was going to cause a problem. But then maybe he did that to everyone who entered the museum.

She glanced around at the large entry area, which featured a ticket counter in the middle, filled with brochures, maps, books, and bookmarks. The place smelled old—like her grandmother's dusty old attic. That's pretty much what a museum was—a big attic full of old, really cool stuff.

As the two teachers and four parent volunteers led the students toward the back of the museum, Cody glanced at some of the exhibits, keeping an eye out for a triangle/eye. She noticed what looked like a dark tunnel off to the side, but the entrance was blocked with a rope and a sign that read,

NO ADMITTANCE. UNDER CONSTRUCTION.

Ms. Stad held up a hand as they reached a door marked CONSERVATION LAB.

"Students, I'm sorry, but it looks like the tunnel Mr. Pike mentioned is closed for repairs."

The students groaned. Cody couldn't help but be disappointed. Even though it was scary, she still wanted to see a real mummy.

"We'll have to come back some other time and see it," Ms. Stad continued. "But today I have a special treat for you. Before we visit the other Egyptian exhibits, we've been invited to the Conservation Lab for a behind-the-scenes peek at some of the museum's most interesting secrets. Not many people get to see this part of the museum, so watch and listen, and perhaps you'll be able to solve those puzzles Mr. Pike and I gave you earlier."

The students shuffled through the door and into a large, brightly lit area that was filled with tall tables, stools, and supplies. Cody recognized Ms. Cassatt, again dressed all in black and again wearing the Eye of Horus pendant around her neck.

She was talking to a man in a white lab coat, wearing latex gloves and thick magnifying glasses. He sat perched at a table, hunched over what looked like an identical copy of the pendant Ms. Cassatt wore. The only difference was this Eye of Horus was blue, while Ms. Cassatt's Eye was green, matching her eyes. The man dusted off the Eye, sprayed it with something, and set it aside. Cody wrinkled her nose at the smell of chemicals wafting around the room. She hoped it wasn't the smell of mummified bodies.

The man stood up, removed the glasses, and turned to the students. Under the open lab coat, he wore a T-shirt featuring a lion's body with a human head, plus faded blue jeans and Birkenstock sandals. His hair was black and spiky like Quinn's, he had black eyebrows and dark stubble on his face, and he sported a gold nose ring. Cody noticed he had a tattoo that encircled his neck. She recognized some of the symbols from class: an upside-down hook, a square, a zigzag, a cup. His tattoo was in hieroglyphic writing.

Code Buster's Key and Solution found on pp. 172, 174.

Hmm, she thought, quietly pulling out the hieroglyphic decoder card Ms. Stad had given the students. *I wonder what that means?*

Chapter 4

Using her decoder card, Cody began to translate the symbols tattooed on the man's neck. The first letter was familiar—it was the same first letter of the word they'd had for homework: *s* for *steganography*. When she was finished decoding the rest of the symbols, she recognized the word from one of Ms. Stad's lessons. In fact, it was the name of the human-headed lion on the man's T-shirt.

Ms. Stad interrupted her thoughts. "Students, you remember the curator of the museum, Ms. Cassatt, who visited our classroom? And this is Dr. Malik Jordan. He's an art conservationist and forgery expert here at the Rosicrucian Egyptian Museum. He's going to tell us a little about how he restores damaged art and how to spot a forgery. Please give Dr. Jordan your full attention."

The students applauded as Dr. Jordan gave a slight bow. Meanwhile, Ms. Cassatt stepped back and watched as he addressed the group. Cody noticed one of the security guards—Simon Wood—standing in the shadows at the back. The frown had not left his face. She wondered where the other guard was.

"Thank you kindly, students from Berkeley Cooperative Middle School! Welcome to my laboratory. I'd like to show you a few things I do here that help preserve antique paintings, sculptures, and artifacts, so they won't be further damaged by age or improper handling."

Cody's mind wandered as the man talked about his techniques, and she glanced around the room to see if she could spot any mummies. But as soon as he mentioned the word *forgery*, her ears pricked up.

"Believe it or not," Dr. Jordan said, "almost every priceless painting in every museum has at one time or another been copied. By studying paints, brushwork, tools, and even wormholes in panels, we can tell whether a painting is authentic or a forgery. And surprisingly, many forgers are so proud of their fakes that they leave a 'calling card'—a symbol or message bragging about their expertise."

"Cool!" "Wow!" "Sweet!" the students whispered.

Dr. Jordan continued. "Forgers often try to 'age' their copies by dipping them in special chemicals. But we can usually spot those, too. See, we also use chemicals to determine what the paints are made of. Sometimes, we use X-rays, infrared, carbon dating, and even computers. The work I do is sort of the *CSI* of art—we use a lot of forensic techniques."

Awesome! Cody thought. These people were doing police-type stuff, just like her mom, only they were doing it to find out if art was real or fake.

"Have you ever discovered a forgery at the museum?" Jack asked.

"No—" Ms. Cassatt was quick to answer.

Dr. Jordan interrupted her. "That's not quite true, Mirabel. We had one guy try to sell us a fake piece of jewelry, but it didn't take long to figure out it was a forgery. Of course, that doesn't mean that there aren't more lurking around here somewhere. Perhaps we just haven't found them yet."

Wouldn't it be awesome to uncover a forgery? Cody thought. But if this expert hadn't found one in his own museum yet, she and the other Code Busters probably wouldn't either. Oh, well. She'd stick to cracking codes for now.

Melissa from Cody's class raised her hand. "Why do people copy the paintings? Why don't they just buy them if they like them?"

Dr. Jordan smiled at the girl. "Mainly because the originals cost too much. That's why some art lovers settle for a fake and pretend it's real. Other times, forgers pass off the fakes as real and sell them for a lot of money. And sometimes they even switch the real ones for the fake ones, thinking no one will ever discover the truth. Forgers can make a lot of money by copying and selling their work to art galleries, museums, and private collectors. Believe it or not, one forger even tried to create a fake mummy!"

The room filled with whispers. Cody shivered.

"What about the Mummy's Curse?" Matt the Brat called out without raising his hand.

While Ms. Stad shot Matt a look, Dr. Jordan grinned at him. Cody had a feeling he got that question a lot.

Before he could answer, Ms. Cassatt stepped forward, holding her Eye of Horus pendant in her hand. "I think we better get back to the topic—"

Dr. Jordan turned to her. "It's okay, Mirabel. Mummies are fascinating, and there are a lot of superstitions associated with them." He returned his attention to the students. "I'm sorry to disappoint you, but there's no such thing as a Mummy's Curse. Only in the movies. That rumor started when an archaeologist named Howard Carter discovered the tomb of King Tutankhamun—King Tut—back in 1922. It was quite an exciting find. Imagine entering an Egyptian tomb filled with treasures that were hidden for over three thousand years!"

Cody heard mumbling from her classmates.

"What happened?" asked Lauren.

"Well, after the tomb was opened, they found not only gold and treasure but walls inscribed with curses. They were probably written to scare away tomb robbers, but the writing promised that desecraters would die by snakebite, scorpions, or crocodiles. As a matter of fact, several people who were at the opening did die in the next ten years. But it was mostly of natural causes."

Ryan raised his hand. "I heard there were deadly gases in the tombs and that's why everyone died."

Dr. Jordan shook his head. "While it's true that some of the ancient mummies carried mold, scientists say there were no deadly gases and the mold wasn't dangerous. But I'll admit, I do love movies where the mummies come back to life. They give me chills!"

"Why can't we go in the tunnel and see the mummy?" Matt shouted out.

Ms. Cassatt stepped forward. "I'm sorry, but that exhibit is . . . undergoing maintenance." Cody noticed she looked uncomfortable answering the question. "It . . . could be dangerous."

"But that's what I really want to see," Matt argued. "It's supposed to be like a real pyramid in there. And I heard the mummy is awesome, all decayed and stuff."

Dr. Jordan took over for Ms. Cassatt, who suddenly seemed tongue-tied. "The truth is, they found vermin in there—rats—so Ms. Cassatt has called in exterminators to treat the problem. You wouldn't want to run into one of those nasty little creatures in that dark tunnel, would you?" He grinned. It seemed as if he enjoyed giving the students a little thrill.

"Dr. Jordan," Ms. Cassatt said, "I don't think the students need to know all of that."

Dr. Jordan rubbed the tattoo on the back of his neck, as if Ms. Cassatt had suddenly given him a pain there.

Matt the Brat spoke again without being called on. "What does your tattoo say?"

"Matthew!" Ms. Stad snapped at the boy, but

again Dr. Jordan grinned. He didn't seem to mind being asked a personal question.

"You noticed, eh? These are hieroglyphs that spell out a word. I understand you students have been studying the hieroglyphic symbols."

They nodded.

"Good. So, does anyone know what my tattoo says?"

Cody and several others raised their hands. Dr. Jordan called on Cody.

"Sphinx?" she said.

"Correct! Do you know what a sphinx is?"

"It's that big statue in Egypt that looks like a lion with a human head," Cody said. "There's a picture of it on your shirt."

Dr. Jordan pulled open his lab coat to show the students his T-shirt. "You noticed that, too. Very good. Yes, the Great Sphinx of Giza, also known as 'the Terrifying One,' is the largest monolithic statue in the world. It was probably built around 2500 BC. Unfortunately, even with all that we've learned about Egyptian history, we still don't know much more about the Sphinx—why it was built, what it means. It's quite a mixture of science, art, and mystery. You've heard of the Mummy's Curse, so I assume you've also heard the Riddle of the Sphinx?"

The students shook their heads.

"Ah, well. Some say the Sphinx guarded the entrance to the city of Thebes," Dr. Jordan explained. "Travelers who wanted to go inside were asked a riddle before entering."

"What was the riddle?" M.E. asked.

Ms. Stand shot her a warning look, and M.E. blushed.

"You want to try to solve it, eh?" Dr. Jordan grinned. "Well, here it is: Which creature walks on four legs in the morning, two legs in the afternoon, and three legs in the evening? But I must warn you. If you can't answer the riddle, the Sphinx will devour you!"

The kids laughed.

"Does anyone know the answer?" he asked.

Matt the Brat's hand shot up. "*A Tyrannosaurus rex?*"

Dr. Jordan shook his head. Cody rolled her eyes. Ms. Stad grimaced.

"A lizard," said another kid. "'Cause it has four legs, and then it can lose two legs, but then maybe it only grows back one . . ." The boy drifted off, lost in his own answer.

"Nope," said Dr. Jordan. "Give up?"

The students nodded.

"It's *man*—or woman. First man crawls on four legs as a baby, then he walks on two feet as an adult, and finally he uses a cane when he gets old."

The kids groaned.

"That was hard! I would never have guessed that," M.E. said.

Dr. Jordan raised a dark eyebrow. "Then I'm afraid, young lady, you'd have been devoured."

The class burst into laughter. When the roar died down, Dr. Jordan turned back to Cody. "As for the tattoo, I chose the word *sphinx* because it's a mysterious riddle, much like ancient Egyptian artifacts still are. And much like art continues to be."

"I think we're about out of time," Ms. Cassatt said.

"We need to let Dr. Jordan get back to his work."

"All right, students in my class," Mr. Pike said. "Did you find the spider and all the thirteens on the dollar bill homework assignment I gave you?"

Luke and Quinn raised their hands, along with several others from Mr. Pike's class. The boys held up their homework sheets, which displayed the hidden objects, all circled in red.

"Great! Whoever found the most thirteens connected with the bill and U.S. history wins a make-your-own-mummy kit from the museum store."

Mr. Pike's students counted up their finds. Luke and Quinn tied for first place. Quinn read his list: "Thirteen original colonies, signers of the Declaration of Independence, stripes on the flag, steps on the pyramid, letters in *E pluribus unum*, stars above the eagle, bars on the shield, leaves on the olive branch, fruits, and arrows."

"Nice work, boys! Congratulations!" Mr. Pike said. "You win the make-your-own-mummy kit."

Ms. Stadelhofer turned to her students. "How about my class? Did any of you figure out the hidden message in the triangle/eye picture that I gave you for today's homework?"

A few students offered their guesses, everything from "eye of the mountain" to "eye love triangles" to "eye-gyptian pyramid."

Ms. Stad shook her head. "I don't think those are quite right. Keep thinking. Meanwhile, I have a new puzzle for you to solve." She passed out a map of the museum layout to each student. To Cody, the map resembled the inside of a pyramid, with pathways winding around in a maze.

"In a few minutes, you may explore the four rooms of the museum," Ms. Stad said. "But first you need to decode the anagrams below. Once you've done that, then you must locate each name and mark it on the map. You'll also find a clue hidden near each one. Collect the clues, then try to decode the final message. At the end of the hour, bring the map with your answers to the gift shop for a prize. Good luck!"

Sweet! Cody thought. Ms. Stad even made visiting a museum a mysterious adventure!

*   *   *   *   *

Under the watchful eye of the two security guards, who seemed to be everywhere, the Code Busters found a spot in the lobby and sat down to decode the message. There were ten anagrams, each with a brief definition as a clue. The Code Busters went to work on the puzzle.

1. *Sisi* – "Goddess of love and magic, with a throne on her head."

2. *Numa* – "Hidden one who takes the form of a hawk."

3. *Subain* – "Protector of mummies from evil forces, in the form of a jackal."

4. *Bettas* – "Cat goddess in the shape of the moon."

5. *Shour* – "Falcon god in the shape of a triangle with an eye in the middle."

6. *Atam* – "Goddess of truth and justice, wearing an ostrich feather on her head."

7. *Rissio* – "King of eternal man, in the form of a mummy."

8. *Themesk* – "Goddess of war and healing, with a lion's head."

9. *Skobe* – "Crocodile-headed river god."

10. *Hotth* – "Lord of the moon and time and inventor of writing."

Code Buster's Solution found on p. 175.

After Cody deciphered two of the anagrams—*Isis* and *Horus*—she realized these were taken from her spelling words. The rest took a little more work, but soon the kids had a list of names they were to find in the museum. The first clue led them to a sculpture that looked like a hawk. First, the Code Busters noted the location on the map. Then, they checked the wall behind the object and found a sticky note written in hieroglyphs.

"An arm?" M.E. said. "What's that supposed to mean? The letter *e*?"

The kids used their hieroglyphic decoder cards to finish deciphering the word and wrote the translation on the back of their maps.

Cody shrugged. "We need more clues. Let's keep going."

Winding through the labyrinthine corridors, the kids continued to hunt for the objects on the list. At each spot, they found another clue and jotted it down. Soon they had all ten clues.

1. ⌐⌐
2. ⌐⌐
3. ⌐
4. ⌐
5. ⌐
6. ⌐
7. ⌐⌐
8. ⌐
9. ⌐
10. ⌐

They sat down on a bench in the lobby and reviewed the clues, using the hiero-alpha decoder card.

"Okay," Quinn said, "first there's an arm, which is the letter *e*. Then there's a square turning inward, the symbol for the letter *h*. . . ." He continued reading the rest of the list until they had a series of what seemed to be random letters. "So what does this all mean?"

"I'm stuck," Luke said, shaking his head.

"I don't get it either," M.E. added.

Cody took a deep breath. She hated giving up, especially when it came to code busting. After all, this was her passion.

Cody looked at the letters. "Maybe it's an anagram," Luke said. Luke and his *grand-mère* loved to solve anagrams together.

Cody rearranged the letters. *"Youre foshe?"* she said aloud. *"Hoo see fury?"* She tried several more combinations. Finally, one word made sense: "Horus!"

"That's it!" Quinn said. They quickly completed the two other words.

Cody sat up, excited. "Talk about steganography. The answer has been right in front of us the whole time!"

Code Buster's Solution found on p. 175.

Chapter 5

"S o, did we solve the puzzle?" M.E. asked.

"The Eye of Horus," Quinn said. "That has to be it."

"I guess so," Cody said, looking over the answer, "but it seems like something's missing. It was almost too easy."

"Well, there's only one way to find out," Luke said. "We show it to Ms. Stad and see what she says."

The kids found their teacher in the museum lobby, checking the papers of a few other students who had also completed the puzzle. Ms. Stad read over their paper, but instead of a prize, they each received a small card with a question mark on the front. Cody took her card and flipped it over. On the other side was another drawing of an eye, but this one looked different from the one in the triangle. It was fancy, with black strokes around the lid, a long eyebrow, a curl coming out of the eye, and what seemed like a tear. It reminded her of the necklace Ms. Cassatt was wearing.

On the bottom of the picture were the words "How many Eyes of Horus can you find in the museum?"

Cody read aloud the note written underneath the drawing. "The Eye of Horus was often found carved or drawn on an amulet, and was used for protection, power, and health. If you look closely, you'll see the design is actually made up of seven different hiero-glyphs used for mathematical measurement."

"Interesting," Quinn said, after Cody finished reading. "Well, let's go see if we can find all the Eyes."

They returned to the first of the four rooms and began scouting for Eyes of Horus. It wasn't an easy task, since there seemed to be Eyes all over the place. After locating as many as they could find, the Code Busters marked them on their papers and headed for the next room. Finally, in the last room, Cody spotted another Eye of Horus artifact, but there was something odd about this one. It sat alone on a pedestal inside a clear case the size of an upended shoe box.

"This looks almost exactly like the necklace Ms. Cassatt has on," Cody said. "And like the Eye of Horus Dr. Jordan was working on. Only the iris is green like Ms. Cassatt's necklace, not blue like the one in the lab."

Cody tapped one side of the case that protected the valuable artifact. A small side door popped open.

Cody jerked her hand back and glanced around.

"Whoa!" Quinn said, staring at the case.

"What's wrong?" M.E. asked.

"The side of the case—it opened!" Cody said. She glanced around for security guards, but they were nowhere in sight.

"Uh-oh. You busted it," Luke said, his eyes wide.

"I did not!" Cody protested. She tapped the door to close it, but instead it ricocheted and bounced back open again. "Somebody left it unlocked!"

"Seriously?" M.E. said, staring at the Eye.

"Dude!" Luke said. "Anybody could just walk in here and steal this thing!"

M.E. reached up as if in a trance and stuck her hand inside the case. She lifted the artifact before Cody could stop her. "It's so beautiful."

"Put that back!" Cody whispered to M.E. She glanced around to see if anyone was watching, but the other students were busy hunting for other Eyes and didn't seem to notice them. "You're going to get us in trouble!"

To Cody's horror, M.E. flipped over the Eye of Horus and studied it up-close. "I just want to look for a moment. Look, there's something written on the bottom!"

M.E. raised her palm and showed the tiny carved drawings to the others.

"Hieroglyphs!" Cody whispered, suddenly excited to see the hidden inscription.

"What's it say?" Luke asked.

Cody pulled out her decoder card and quickly translated the symbols:

Code Buster's Key and Solution found on pp. 172, 175.

"How weird," Cody said. "What's it supposed to mean?"

Quinn spoke up. "'An eye for an eye' means that when someone hurts another person, he or she gets a similar punishment—or something like that."

"That's weird," M.E. said. "I wonder why it says that."

"Guys, watch out!" Luke whispered. "One of the security guards just came into the room. You better put that thing back! Fast! Or he'll think we're trying to steal it."

The kids huddled around the display case to block

the view of anyone nearby. M.E. set the Eye back on its small stand, and Cody forced the slightly warped door closed.

Just then a voice came from behind them. "So, what are you students up to?"

Cody jumped. The Code Busters spun around to find Dr. Jordan staring down at them. He seemed to have appeared out of nowhere. Cody thought she saw an odd smile on his face, as if he knew what they'd been doing. Had the security guard said something to him? Or had it been her imagination, and her guilty conscience?

"We were . . . just looking at this Eye," she said. "It's pretty cool."

"Ah, yes. That's one of the artifacts I was working on this morning. It's beautiful, isn't it, now that it's all cleaned up and back on its pedestal?"

M.E. started to ask, "What does the writing on the bot—"

Cody cut her off. "—on the bottle . . . over there—" She pointed wildly across the room, hoping at least one of the displays contained an antique bottle, since she'd seen several throughout the museum. They couldn't let Dr. Jordan know they'd opened the display case and touched the Eye. If anything happened to it, they'd be blamed.

Cody led Dr. Jordan over to another case where a few students lingered, found a bottle that happened to be covered in hieroglyphs, and pointed to it. Moments later, more students entered the room, distracting Dr. Jordan from the display case. The Code Busters quietly backed out of the room.

"That was close," Cody whispered.

"Sorry," M.E. said quietly. "I almost gave us away!"

"No problem," Quinn said to M.E. He turned to Cody. "Good thinking, Cody, distracting him like that."

"Should we tell someone that the door on the case is loose?" Luke asked. "I mean, anybody could steal that Eye of Horus with that door unlocked."

Cody thought for a moment. "Good point. How about we tell Ms. Stad, and she can tell Ms. Cassatt, since she's in charge of the museum? Hopefully, Ms. Stad will leave us out of it."

Luke and Quinn nodded, but M.E. was staring at her hand, frowning.

"M.E., what's wrong?" Cody asked.

She held up her hand. "Look!"

Cody examined her friend's fingers, then sniffed them. M.E.'s fingertips looked as if they'd been smudged with brown ink, and they smelled like chemicals.

"How did you get your hand so dirty?" Cody asked.

M.E. shrugged. "I don't know. All I did was pick up that artifact. I don't remember touching anything else."

Cody looked at her three code-busting friends. While the other students stood across the room listening to Dr. Jordan talk about one of the artifacts, Cody stole over to the case again. She glanced around, then pulled open the unlocked door, reached in, and ran her index finger over the top of the Eye. Removing her hand from the case, she closed the door, then held up her hand.

Her fingertip was brown. The same shade of brown as the amulet.

"Guys," she whispered. "I don't think the color is supposed to come off like that."

M.E. checked her hand again, then looked at the others.

"Do you think that Eye is a fake?" Luke asked.

Cody shrugged. "What do we do? If we tell the museum people we touched it, we could get in trouble. But if it's a fake, wouldn't they want to know? The forger could be a thief, and get away with stealing valuable art."

"That writing on the bottom was weird," M.E. said. "An eye for an *i*?"

"Shh!" Quinn said. "Dr. Jordan is watching us again. I'm sure he thinks we're up to something. We need to move."

Cody turned around and saw the museum guy staring at them strangely. A chill ran down her back. "Come on, it's time to turn in our assignments to Ms. Stad. We'll figure out what to do during lunch. Follow me."

Cody led her friends out of the room and into the lobby, where other students had already gathered with their teachers. Luke and Quinn joined Mr. Pike's group, while Cody and M.E. headed for Ms. Stad's class. When all the students were seated on the floor, Ms. Stad asked, "So, did everyone find all of the Eyes of Horus in the museum?"

Hands shot up.

"How many did you find, Ryan?" she asked the blond kid with glasses, sitting in the middle.

"Eleven!"

"Good," Ms. Stad said. "Anyone else find a different number?"

"Our group found twelve," said Stephanie.

"Nice," Ms. Stad said. "Anyone else?"

M.E. raised her hand. "We found thirteen."

"Wow!" exclaimed Ms. Stad. "Are you sure?"

M.E. nodded and held up her paper.

"Well, believe it or not, our parent volunteers only found twelve when they counted them earlier," Ms. Stad said. "I guess your group found one we missed. Hmm. I wonder if the number *thirteen* is a coincidence."

Cody remembered the number of thirteens they'd

found on the dollar bill. Interesting how that number kept coming up.

"Did you know that many cultures consider *thirteen* a number associated with luck?" Ms. Stad asked. "Some say the Egyptians were the first people to become superstitious about the number. They thought it brought good luck and immortality, and was related to the thirteenth stage of life—the afterlife. Later, the number was associated with death. Other cultures think the number brings bad luck. Can you think of some examples of bad luck associated with *thirteen*?"

Lyla raised her hand. "Friday the thirteenth!"

"Yes!" Ms. Stad said. "Some people believe that's an unlucky day."

Bradley raised his hand. "My dad's office building doesn't have a thirteenth floor because it's supposed to be bad luck. It just goes from twelve to fourteen."

"Great example," Ms. Stad said. "Many hotels, apartment buildings, and office buildings don't have a thirteenth floor. Isn't that interesting?"

The students grinned and nodded.

"By the way," Ms. Stad continued, "many of you students are thirteen years old. How many of you think it's a lucky number?"

A few hands went up. But Cody was having trouble paying attention. She looked at the stain on her fingertip and rubbed it with her thumb. The color had dried and wouldn't come off.

Why is there fresh paint or ink on that artifact? And why is the case loose? Did a thief really steal the Eye of Horus and replace it with a fake?

And if so, then who?

Cody thought Dr. Jordan was the most likely person. He was the one working on a similar artifact in the conservation room. He had access to the displays in the museum. Plus, he knew all about creating forgeries. And he seemed to enjoy riddles, like that hieroglyphic tattoo on his neck. "An eye for an *i*" sounded like a riddle to Cody.

He'd also been watching the Code Busters when they gathered around that plastic case. Cody wondered if he had ink stains on his fingertips. No, she remembered he'd been wearing latex gloves. But Ms. Cassatt said he was an expert on forgeries. . . .

"Cody?" Ms. Stad said, interrupting her thoughts.

M.E. nudged her and whispered, "She asked you a question."

"Oh, sorry, Ms. Stadelhofer. What did you say?" Cody said.

"I asked you a riddle. 'If you see my face, you can see twelve but not thirteen. What am I?'"

Cody tried to think. A face? Without thirteen? It made no sense. Hands shot up around her. She finally shrugged and said, "I . . . I don't know."

Ms. Stad called on Lyla, who said, "A clock!"

"Correct! Students, I want you to keep your eye on the clock. It's time for lunch—and more conundrums, enigmas, and riddles. Please take a handout, then gather your lunch bags, go outside to the courtyard, and return in half an hour with your solutions to these questions. After you've solved them, we'll talk about how mummies are made—and more." She smiled mysteriously as she passed out a sheet of paper to each student.

Cody and the other Code Busters headed outside and found a bench where they could eat their
lunches. While Quinn, Luke, and M.E. read over the
questions and brainstormed answers, Cody noticed
the two guards talking to each other. She overheard
the man say to the woman, ". . . losing money if they
don't get that tunnel cleaned out . . . may have to
close . . ."

She wondered if the museum was in some kind
of trouble. Was the tunnel really that important for
attracting visitors?

"Earth to Cody!" M.E. said, bringing her back to
the moment. "Come on. We need help solving these."

Cody blinked several times. "Sorry. I just can't
help thinking about that unlocked case and the Eye
of Horus inside."

"We'll deal with that when we're done with the
assignment, okay?" Quinn said. "We got the first
one—it was easy. But we're stuck on the second one."

Cody read over the first coded question written in
hieroglyphs to see what she missed:

1. 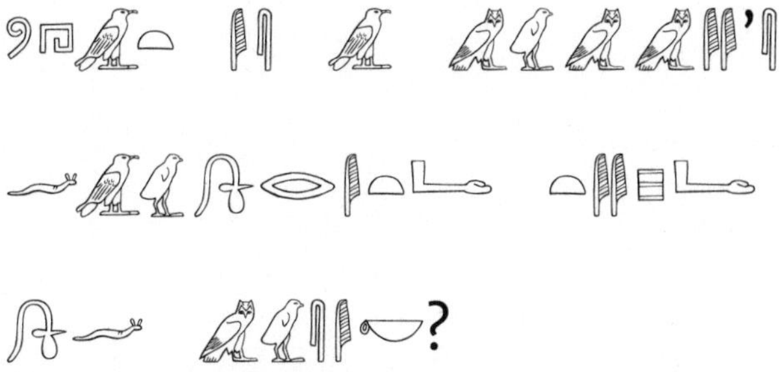 𓅃𓊪𓅃𓉐 𓏏𓏥 𓅃 𓅃𓄿𓅃𓅃𓏥'𓏭

𓂝𓅃𓄿𓇋𓍯�◯𓇋�◯𓂋 �◯𓏥𓐍𓂋

𓇋𓂝 𓅃𓄿𓏏𓏭𓏤◯?

"Rap music?" Luke suggested. "Get it? *Wrap* and *rap*?" They wrote down the answer on their handouts. Cody liked jokes and riddles because they played with words and had double meanings, although at the moment, she was finding it hard to concentrate. Quinn read the rest of the questions aloud and they all jotted down the answers.

2. 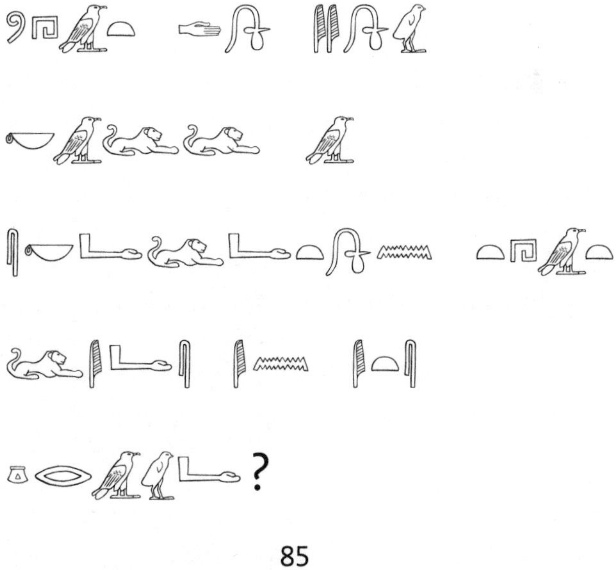 𓅃𓊪𓅃𓉐 𓂝𓇋 𓏤𓏤𓇋𓏏𓄿

𓂋◯𓃭𓃭𓃭 𓅃

𓏭𓂋�◯𓃭𓂝𓇋𓈖〰〰 𓐍𓊪𓅃𓉐

𓃭𓏏𓂋𓏭 𓏭〰〰 𓏭𓂝𓏭

𓐠◯𓅃𓅃𓂋?

85

3.

4.

5.

6.

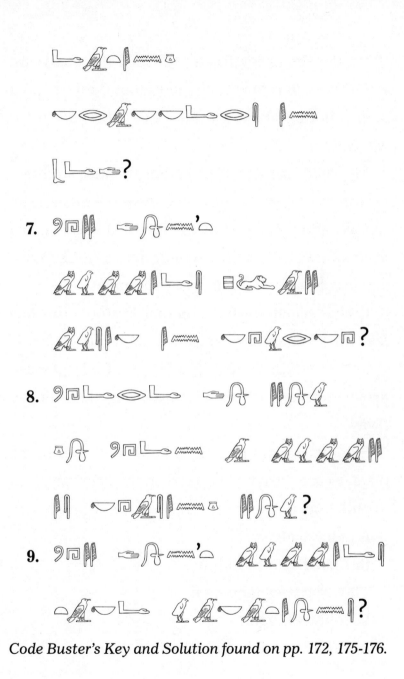

7.

8.

9.

Code Buster's Key and Solution found on pp. 172, 175-176.

By the time they finally finished the questions, it was time to return to the museum. Cody couldn't stop thinking about the fake Eye. She *had* to tell Ms. Stad.

Ms. Stad and Mr. Pike called the kids to attention in the lobby. As Ms. Stad gave the answers to the assignment, the students groaned and laughed at answers. Then it was time to return to the Conservation Lab and learn about mummies.

Cody decided to check on that Eye of Horus one last time before she talked to Ms. Stad, so while the other students filed into the lab, Cody glanced around to see if anyone was watching, then slipped away.

She tiptoed into the empty room and over to the display case. Placing her hand on the door, she tried to pull it open.

It didn't budge.

She tried again. Nothing.

Then she tried tapping it.

It was stuck tight.

It was locked now. But who had locked it?

The thief, covering his tracks?

If so, how could she and the other Code Busters prove it?

Cody pulled out her cell phone and took a picture of the object . . . just in case.

Chapter 6

Dr. Jordan was in the middle of talking to the students about mummification when Cody slipped into the back of the workroom. Matt the Brat spotted her, and made a face. She ignored him. Cody saw Ms. Cassatt fiddling with her pendant again, while she watched from the sidelines, her eyes darting around the room. Cody noticed how fidgety Ms. Cassatt seemed, while Dr. Jordan appeared completely at ease.

Strange, Cody thought, then she returned

her attention to the presentation.

Dr. Jordan stood behind the counter where, earlier, he'd been cleaning the Eye of Horus amulet. In front of him lay a small wooden container the size of a shoe box, covered with faded hieroglyphs that looked as if they had lost their vibrant colors over time.

Cody shivered. She wasn't sure she wanted to see what was in the box after all.

Too late.

Dr. Jordan lifted the top and tilted the box toward the students. Cody glanced inside and saw the small mummified body of a cat. It looked black, bony, and stiff—and totally creeped her out.

"This is Ta-Miewet," Dr. Jordan announced proudly, as if he were introducing an old friend. "He's a mummified cat who was buried with his owner about six thousand years ago. Back then, Egyptians thought cats were magical and could protect them. They even adorned their cats with expensive, ornate jewelry. Believe it or not, all domesticated cats are descendants of Egyptian cats—even yours."

Cody thought of her cat, Punkin. Was he magical? Did he protect her? *No,* she decided. *Just another superstition.*

M.E. whispered in her ear, "You need to get some earrings for Punkin!"

Cody smiled at how ridiculous that sounded. But it was definitely something that M.E. would do for her pets. She was a big fan of jewels, sequins, and glitter.

"Would you like to know how mummies are made?" Dr. Jordan asked.

The group responded eagerly. Cody's stomach tightened.

"All right, but this might be a bit gruesome." He grinned. The light glinted off his nose ring.

"First, the body is washed and cast with magical spells for protection. All the organs are removed, except for the heart. Wine is poured over the body to disinfect it. The organs are covered with salt and baking soda, and set out to dry. Then they're placed in vessels called canopic jars. The body is perfumed and wrapped up tightly, and good-luck amulets are added. Finally, the body is placed in a coffin—called a sarcophagus—that is often painted to look like the deceased and adorned with hieroglyphs. Once the process is finished, the body can stay intact for centuries."

"Why did they do all that?" asked Jodie from Mr. Pike's class. "Why not just bury them like we do now?"

"The Egyptians believed this process would ensure them a happy afterlife," Dr. Jordan said.

"Weird," Jodie mumbled.

"Well, certainly different from our customs today," Dr. Jordan said. "The Egyptians never cremated bodies. They preserved them in preparation for the afterlife. And not everyone was allowed in. You had to serve some purpose, like the pharaoh. They believed he became a type of god after he died."

Dr. Jordan pointed to the mouth of the cat. "After the mummy was prepared, a priest touched its mouth with a blade, to ensure the mummy could breathe and speak in the afterlife. This part of the ceremony was called reanimation."

"I saw a movie about that," Matt said. "This mummy came back to life and started going after all the people."

Dr. Jordan didn't seem to hear Matt. He continued explaining the burial ritual. "After they recited prayers and burned incense, the mummy was placed inside the pyramid, along with lots of food, clothes, jewelry, and even furniture, to make the afterlife more comfortable. Then the pyramid was sealed, never to be entered again. That is, until tomb raiders came along." Several students murmured excitedly at the mention of tomb raiders.

"Any questions?" Dr. Jordan asked the group.

When no one raised a hand, Cody started thinking about the open display case and the still-wet coloring on the Eye of Horus. The Code Busters didn't have any proof that the Eye was a fake—only circumstantial evidence. Her dad was a lawyer and he'd talked about circumstantial evidence a lot. Basically, it meant that there were clues leading to a fact, but nothing concrete that could absolutely *prove* that fact. It was like if your little sister had a chocolate milk mustache but swore she didn't take the last carton. It was possible that she got her mustache drinking the milk at a neighbor's house. That's circumstantial proof. But if her *fingerprints* were found on the fridge and the empty carton, that would be what her dad called "corroborating evidence." That plus the mustache might prove the crime.

Fingerprints.

That gave Cody an idea.

If she could prove that Dr. Jordan's fingerprints were on the Eye and the case, wouldn't that mean he could have switched the artifacts?

No, she decided glumly. He obviously touched the Eye and the case when he went to get the amulet for cleaning. In fact, his fingerprints would be all over the place.

And besides, she still didn't know for sure if the Eye in the case was real or not. She thought it was a fake because of the brown stain that came off on their fingers. Now that the case was relocked, the Code Busters couldn't even prove it had ever been open.

That brown coloring had to be proof of something. But Dr. Jordan could argue that the girls must have touched something on the work counter in his lab.

Thoughts bounced around in Cody's head like pebbles during a sandstorm. She was getting nowhere. All this talk of mummies, and forgeries, was feeding her already active imagination.

"Students!" Ms. Stad called out after Dr. Jordan was finished answering questions about mummies. "Let's give Dr. Jordan a round of applause for his wonderful presentation! That was fascinating."

The group clapped enthusiastically.

"I still want to see a real mummy," Matt grumbled. Ms. Stad hushed him.

"Now, turn in your papers, if you haven't already. Then you're free to go to the gift shop. Those of you who won the prize, come see me. I'll have something special for the group that solved the most puzzles when we gather in half an hour."

Ms. Stad gave each of the Code Busters a rolled-up sheet of paper. Cody unrolled hers and smiled at the painting inside. "These are hand-painted pictures on real papyrus," Ms. Stad explained. "Each one is different."

Cody held hers up for the others to see. It was a painting of the Eye of Horus. M.E. unrolled hers to find a painting of a sarcophagus. Luke showed his—a picture of a pyramid. And Quinn got a picture of the Rosetta Stone.

"Awesome," Quinn said. The others nodded, pleased with their prizes. They rolled them back up and stuck them carefully in their backpacks. As Ms. Stad stood there talking to some other students, Cody opened another compartment in her backpack and pulled out her Code Busters notebook. She wrote a message in Morse code, added her code name at the end, then tore it out and passed it to M.E. It read:

```
--   .   .   -     --   .   ..   -.

.--  ---  .-.  -.-  .-.  ---  ---  --

-.-.  ---  -..  .     .-.  .  -..
```

Code Buster's Key and Solution found on pp. 170, 176.

M.E. read the note, then passed it on to Quinn, who passed it to Luke. While Ms. Stad and the other students browsed the gift shop for Egyptian trinkets to buy, the Code Busters slipped away and headed for the workroom in the back of the museum.

Cody glanced around to make sure no one saw them. She tried the knob. It opened. She waved the others to follow her inside.

The room appeared empty. No sign of Dr. Jordan.

Cody whispered, "If the Eye of Horus in that case is fake, then maybe the real Eye is in here somewhere. Dr. Jordan could have hidden it for safe-keeping, planning to come back for it later when the museum closes. Maybe he's going to sneak it out and take it with him when he leaves for the day, like that thief Ms. Cassatt told us about. We have to find the real Eye if we're going to prove that the one in the case is a fake."

"Cody, we could search this place all day and not find anything," M.E. whined. "There are too many places to hide something that small. It could be any-where."

"She's right," Quinn said. "We have to think about this logically. Where would we hide something like that if we stole it?"

Cody looked around at all the tables, cupboards, shelves, and desks. There was no way they'd find the Eye if it was hidden in this room. There were just too many places to search, and no time to do it. This was hopeless. Talk about a riddle that was impossible to solve: Where would you hide an Eye that can't see?

She thought about the riddle that was written on the bottom of the artifact: "an eye for an *i*." Was that a clue? Dr. Jordan said that many forgers were proud of their fakes and left a "calling card"—a symbol or message meant to brag about their expertise, and even possibly identify them. Ms. Cassatt said that like Leonardo da Vinci, one forger used to leave his initials hidden in the artwork. Another one always wrote the names of his children in the picture, and then disguised them. And another used to sign his name, then paint over it so no one could see it. Dr. Jordan said it was detected by using infrared and ultraviolet fluorescent light.

Cody heard Ms. Stad calling all the students from the lobby.

"Uh-oh. Time to go back," she said, disappointed they hadn't solved their mystery. She was just about to follow the others out when she had an idea and ran back to the counter where Dr. Jordan had been working. Behind it was a wastebasket, filled with wrinkled papers, soiled cloths—and latex gloves.

Cody retrieved the pair of gloves from the top of the pile. The fingertips were smudged brown. She stuffed the gloves into her hoodie pocket and returned to the lobby with the others to rejoin their classes.

"Listen up, everyone," Ms. Stad called out. "Mr. Pike and I have reviewed all your answers to the codes, questions, and riddles from earlier. And we have a grand prize winner! The group that had the most correct answers and now gets a sneak peek at the next planned exhibit with Ms. Cassatt is . . . the Code Busters!"

"Yes!" Quinn and Luke's fists shot in the air. Cody and M.E. high-fived each other.

Winning this reward lifted Cody's spirits. At least she and her friends would get to see something the other students wouldn't until their next visit to the museum. She hoped Ms. Cassatt would show them some cool artifacts, and maybe even a mummy.

"Quiet down, please," Ms. Stad continued after her announcement. "Not only did they find the most Eyes of Horus throughout the museum—thirteen, one more than the parent volunteers found, in fact— but they also solved all of the puzzles! Great job!"

Wait a minute, Cody thought. *Something's wrong.* An alarm sounded in her head.

She did the math again to make sure. Ms. Stad said there were originally twelve Eyes. But they had found thirteen. Maybe the parent volunteers didn't count wrong. Maybe another Eye of Horus had been added to the collection. A fake? If so, maybe the real one wasn't hidden in the workroom. Maybe it was hidden right in front of their eyes!

"All right, students," Ms. Stad announced. "Now that Cody, M.E., Quinn, and Luke are back from their preview, it's time to reboard the bus and head back to school. Find your buddy and line up, please."

Cody shot a panicked glance at M.E. It had been cool seeing the upcoming exhibit, but she'd hoped to get a chance to search the museum for the extra Eye. She finger-spelled a message so no one would overhear her:

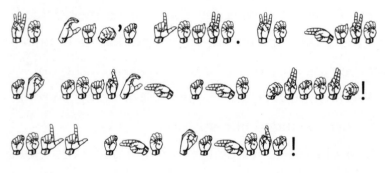

M.E. frowned at her friend and finger-spelled:

Code Buster's Key and Solution found on pp. 171, 176.

Cody ignored her friend and signed, "Hurry!" then went to find her teacher while M.E. passed the message along to the boys.

"Ms. Stad!" Cody called, elbowing through the crowd of students who were lining up for the bus.

"What is it, Cody?" Ms. Stad asked, as she counted heads. "You and M.E. need to get in line. We're leaving in five minutes."

"I . . . I," Cody stammered. She couldn't tell Ms. Stad her suspicions without proof. Her teacher would think she was crazy. But she had to check out the rooms again to make sure she was right. "I . . . left my cell phone in one of the rooms. I need to find it! M.E. and Luke and Quinn said they'd help me. It'll only take us a few seconds. We'll be right back!"

Before Ms. Stad could respond, Cody raced to meet her friends at the entrance of the Daily Life room. She hoped her little white lie would buy her enough time.

"Find all of the Eyes you can!" Cody ordered the puzzled Code Busters. She held up the cell phone snapshot of the Eye that was in the unlocked case. "Look for one that's the same as this."

"Why are we doing this?" M.E. asked, while the boys began searching.

"I think there's an extra Eye somewhere that doesn't belong. Remember when we counted the

Eyes and found thirteen, when Stad said the parent volunteers only found twelve? Well, the thirteenth one has got to be the real Eye of Horus, added *after* the parents counted them. If we find it, then maybe we can prove the one in the case is a fake. I think Dr. Jordan hid it with the other artifacts, figuring it would blend in and no one would notice it. I'm sure it's been right in front of our eyes the whole time."

The girls joined the boys in their search, but none of them found a match in the Daily Life room.

"Follow me," Cody said, racing to the Burial Practices room. After a quick but thorough search that turned up nothing, they moved on to the Gods and Religion room, and finally to the Kings and Pharaohs room.

And then, inside a case filled with jewelry worn by Egyptian royalty, Cody spotted a statue of a cat painted with hieroglyphs and covered in jewelry. "Look!" she said, alerting the others. "See that cat?"

M.E. peered into the case. "The one with all the necklaces, and earrings, and a tiara? I wish I had all that stuff. What about it?"

"Look closely."

M.E. blinked. "Wow. I didn't even notice it before."

"What?" Quinn asked.

M.E. pointed. "Look what's hanging around that cat's neck. A bunch of necklaces, including an Eye of Horus!"

"Yes!" Cody said. "And it's identical to the one in the case. It probably wasn't there when the parents checked. I'll bet none of the other kids saw it because that cat is wearing so much jewelry. It just blends in."

Cody held her cell phone picture up to the display case to double-check.

The amulet was identical.

"That's it!" M.E. squealed. "We found it!"

Before Cody could respond, she heard footsteps behind them. She lowered her cell phone and froze.

"Found what?" came a deep voice.

The Code Busters turned around slowly. Standing in the doorway was Dr. Jordan.

There was no smile on his face this time. His eyebrows were drawn together.

"What are you kids doing in here?" he said, ominously, his dark eyes reflecting his sudden dark mood. "I thought you'd left."

Thinking fast, Cody suddenly lifted her arms out like an airplane, then jerked them up to form a giant Y, and finally dropped them down as if framing a full skirt. She was signaling her friends.

Code Buster's Key and Solution found on pp. 171, 176.

They all raced from the room.

Chapter 7

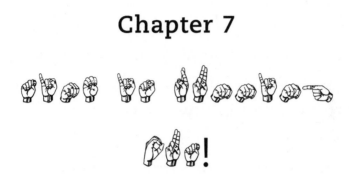

The Code Busters ran up to Ms. Stad and breath-
lessly began to explain the situation.

"The Eye is a fake . . . ," Cody said.

"We found the real one . . . ," M.E. continued.

"We know who switched them . . . ," Luke added.

"He's after us!" Quinn blurted.

"Whoa, whoa!" Ms. Stad said. "Slow down! What
are you talking about? I thought you went into the
museum to look for your phone, Cody."

"I was . . . ," Cody stammered. "I mean, I . . . I was looking for something . . ."

Cody realized she'd been caught in a lie. It was a small lie, but now Ms. Stad might not believe anything else she said.

The teacher crossed her arms and looked at each of the four kids, disappointment etched on her usually pleasant face. But before she could say anything else, a voice bellowed from the doorway of the museum.

"Hold it right there!" Dr. Jordan stood on the top step, his hands on his hips, his dark eyebrows scrunched together menacingly.

Ms. Stad looked up at the man, then back at the kids.

Uh-oh, Cody thought. *We're in deep trouble now.*

Dr. Jordan stepped down and headed for the small group.

"Is something wrong?" Ms. Stad asked him. The Code Busters moved behind her for protection.

Dr. Jordan peered at them before addressing Ms. Stad. "I'll say there is. I believe these kids have something that belongs to the museum. Isn't that right, kids?"

Cody stepped forward, frowning at the accusation. "No, we don't. You're the one who took the real Eye from the case and switched it with a fake."

Dr. Jordan's mouth dropped open. He suddenly looked more puzzled than angry. "What are you talking about? I saw you kids over by the Eye of Horus in the Daily Life room. You were acting very suspicious. When I went to check on the display after you left the room, I found this. It's a fake. Do you kids know anything about this?"

"No," M.E. said. "We thought you took it."

Dr. Jordan frowned at M.E. "What's that on your hands?" he asked.

M.E. turned her hands over to look at them, then quickly put them behind her back.

"Why are your fingertips stained?" Ms. Stad looked at M.E. "What is he talking about, Maria-Elena? What's that on your fingers?" M.E. reluctantly withdrew her hands from behind her back and showed them to Ms. Stad, who inspected them closely. She turned to the other Code Busters. "Let me see your hands, too." Quinn, Luke, and Cody held up their hands. Ms. Stad looked at Cody. "What's that stain on your fingertip?"

By now a crowd of students had gathered around the scene, wide-eyed and openmouthed. Embarrassed by the drama, Cody felt her neck turn hot, and she broke out in a sweat. She almost wished she could crawl into a sarcophagus and disappear.

Quinn began explaining. "Listen, Ms. Stadelhofer. M.E. and Cody got those stains when they touched the fake Eye in that case, but they didn't steal anything. Cody accidentally bumped the case and the door popped open. That's when we realized it wasn't locked. Then M.E. reached in—"

"But I wasn't going to steal the Eye!" M.E. exclaimed, interrupting Quinn. "I just wanted to see it. I put it right back."

"It stained my fingertip, too," Cody said to Ms. Stad. "But I promise, we left the Eye there in the case. We thought maybe it was a fake, so we were going to tell you about the unlocked door, but when we went back to check, the case was locked up again."

"I'm confused," Ms. Stad said, shaking her head. "You found the case open, so you picked up the Eye, and then you put it back and closed the case? Why didn't you tell me *before* you went back to check on it?"

Cody sighed and looked at the others. "We . . . we wanted to make sure it was a fake first. But then it was locked up again, and we had no way to prove anything." She turned to Dr. Jordan. "We thought maybe you switched them, because we saw you working on the Eye in the lab earlier. You said you'd been cleaning it, but when we went back to the lab, we found the gloves you'd been using in the trash. The fingertips were brown, like you'd been staining the Eye."

Dr. Jordan looked down at his fingers.

"We have proof." Cody pulled out the gloves from her hoodie pocket and held them up. "See the stains? You were wearing them when you were working on the Eye. But you weren't wearing them when you replaced the Eye in the case with a fake."

"Let me see those," Dr. Jordan said. Cody hesitated to pass over their proof, but Ms. Stad nodded. Dr. Jordan examined them closely. "These aren't mine."

"But you were wearing gloves earlier," Quinn protested. "And you're an expert in making forgeries. You could easily have made a fake Eye and switched it with the real one."

"Wow," Dr. Jordan finally said. "You kids are something. Well, at least I know you were listening to my lecture. Unfortunately, you've let your imaginations run away with you. I really *was* cleaning that Eye of Horus. I would never use a stain on an authentic artifact. In fact, I thought you kids bought a replica and tried to make it look real by staining it, then switched them. I only checked the case because I saw you kids hovering around it. When I unlocked it, I found the fake."

"Do other staff members at the museum have keys for the displays?" Ms. Stad asked.

Cody looked at her teacher appreciatively. Was she beginning to believe their story?

"A few people . . . ," Dr. Jordan replied, drifting off in thought.

"Is it possible someone else made the switch and accidentally left the case unlocked?" Cody asked.

"I suppose," Dr. Jordan confirmed, "but even so, that doesn't mean the real Eye was replaced with a replica. And the real question is, where is the real Eye now?"

Cody looked at her friends. As if reading her mind, they nodded.

"We have something to show you," Cody said. She glanced at her teacher, who nodded her permission. "Come on!"

Ms. Stad asked Mr. Pike to watch the rest of the students while she accompanied the Code Busters and Dr. Jordan back into the museum. Cody led the way back to the Kings and Pharaohs room, where they'd found the thirteenth Eye draped around the neck of the cat statue. When they reached the display case, Cody peered in.

She gasped.

The Eye was gone!

"But . . . but it was right here!" she stammered.

"What was?" Dr. Jordan asked, looking closely at the display.

"The thirteenth Eye of Horus!" she exclaimed. "It was mixed in with all that jewelry around the cat's neck." She turned to Ms. Stad. "Remember we found thirteen Eyes—one more than you thought?"

Ms. Stad frowned at Cody. "Hmm. Maybe you miscounted after all? I never got a chance to verify your numbers."

"No," Cody said. "We all saw it! It was identical to the other one in the open display case. It was right here!" Suddenly, she wished she'd taken a picture of the cat. That would have been proof.

Dr. Jordan raised an eyebrow but said nothing. Obviously, he thought she was either lying or crazy.

Or maybe there was another reason Dr. Jordan wasn't speaking up.

"What's going on here?" Ms. Cassatt said, approaching the group. The woman seemed to appear out of nowhere. She brushed up against Cody, bumping her slightly, then patted her on the back as if apologizing. "I thought you students were on your way back to school."

Dr. Jordan turned to Ms. Cassatt. "Someone's stolen an Eye of Horus from the Daily Life room. I thought maybe one of the kids—"

"Stolen!" Ms. Cassatt said loudly. "What do you mean?"

Dr. Jordan opened his hand. "I found this Eye in the case. It's a fake. We need to call the police."

"Are you sure it's a fake?" Ms. Cassatt said. "We haven't had a theft here since you started, Malik."

"Of course I'm sure," Dr. Jordan said. "I can run tests on it if you need proof."

"How do you test it?" Cody asked.

He turned to her. "It's very simple, really. When we test an amulet like this, we use a microscope to check for something called natron, which is a mixture of sodium products used in the embalming process. Since most amulets were buried with their owners, who were mummified, we find traces of these minerals on them."

"Give me that!" Ms. Cassatt commanded,

snatching the amulet from Dr. Jordan's palm. She studied it closely. Then she looked up at Dr. Jordan. "I can already tell it's a fake. But if we call the police, word will get out and the museum could lose a great deal of funding. We have to deal with this ourselves. After all, that's why I hired you, Malik."

Cody looked at her friends, sensing something was up with Ms. Cassatt. Protecting the museum's reputation was more important than calling the police and finding the thief? Suddenly, she saw what was right in front of her. She whispered to the Code Busters in phonetic alphabet code: "Charlie, Alpha, Sierra, Sierra, Alpha, Tango, Tango!"

Code Buster's Key and Solution found on pp. 170, 177.

Chapter 8

What do you mean, don't call the police?" Dr. Jordan asked. "A valuable artifact has been stolen from the museum! We can't just do nothing!"

Ms. Cassatt didn't respond. Instead, she turned to Cody, who was still standing next to her.

"I think you took it!" Ms. Cassatt announced.

Cody couldn't believe her ears. "What?"

"Uh-uh!" M.E. said, eyes wide.

"No way!" said Quinn.

"Are you kidding?" Luke said in disbelief.

Cody was too stunned to speak. She stared at Ms. Cassatt, her mouth open. Finally, she blurted, "None of us took it. *We're* the ones who told *you* about the fake!"

"Really?" Ms. Cassatt said, tapping her foot. "The security guard told me you kids were hanging around that case. Empty your pockets."

"I'm telling you," Cody said, protesting, "I didn't take it!"

Ms. Cassatt reached for Cody's hoodie.

Cody moved back. "No way are you touching me!" She turned to Ms. Stad for protection. Her teacher stepped in and blocked Ms. Cassatt.

"Show me what's in your pocket, young lady," Ms. Cassatt commanded.

"This is stupid!" Cody protested, but she reached into her right pocket and pulled out a small piece of paper and a scarab the size of a walnut. She handed everything to Ms. Cassatt. The woman examined the amulet, and then the small paper, which turned out to be the receipt for the scarab. "I bought that in the gift shop! There's the receipt to prove it."

Ms. Cassatt continued to frown as she returned the items to Cody. "Now the other one."

Cody rolled her eyes, but to prove her innocence once and for all, she dug into the left pocket of her hoodie. Withdrawing her hand, she held up her cell phone. "See!"

"Is that all?"

"Yes!" Cody said, raising her hands.

Ms. Cassatt suddenly reached into both of Cody's pockets.

"What are you doing?" Cody squealed.

Ms. Cassatt's frown melted into an evil smile as she withdrew her hands. She opened one palm to reveal the Eye of Horus.

Cody froze. She felt her face flush hot. *This can't be happening*, she thought, glancing at the other Code Busters in panic.

"Well?" Ms. Cassatt said. "I'll bet you don't have a receipt for this! So what do you have to say for yourself, young lady?"

Cody felt her entire body get warm. Her eyes

burned with oncoming tears. *This is a nightmare come true*, she thought. *How did that Eye of Horus get into my pocket?*

M.E. reached for Cody's hand. She began squeezing it off and on. Cody realized M.E. was sending her a message in Morse code. Cody quickly deciphered the short and long squeezes.

... . ⁃ .⁻. .. ⁻.⁻. ⁻.⁻ . ⁻..

⁻.⁻ ⁻ ⁻ ⁻ ⁻ ..⁻

Code Buster's Key and Solution found on pp. 170, 177.

"I'm sure that there's a logical explanation, Ms. Cassatt," Ms. Stad said, wrapping a protective arm around Cody. "These are good kids. They would never steal anything."

"Then how do you explain the fact that this precious artifact was in her pocket?" Ms. Cassatt asked.

"Give the girl a chance to explain," Dr. Jordan said. "Maybe she found it and was planning to return it. And we're not even sure it's authentic. I'd have to run some tests to make sure. May I see it?"

"It's real, all right," Ms. Cassatt said, tightening her grip around the amulet. "I've been working here long enough to know my artifacts." Taking a step back, Ms. Cassatt held up the Eye. "See how the iris is green, just like the one from the Life Studies room? That's very rare. Most Eyes of Horus are blue. This is definitely the one stolen from the case."

Cody blinked at something Ms. Cassatt said. "Green?"

"Correct," Ms. Cassatt said, clutching the artifact tightly again. "Like I said, most of the Eyes of Horus were blue."

"Green," Cody repeated, as if in a trance.

M.E. squeezed Cody's hand again.

-. . -.-. -.- .-.. .- -.-. .

Code Buster's Key and Solution found on pp. 170, 177.

Leave it to M.E. to notice the woman's jewelry! Cody looked up at her accuser. The Eye of Horus pendant was missing from around Ms. Cassatt's neck.

"Where's the necklace you were wearing this

morning when we got to the museum?"

Ms. Cassatt placed her hand on her chest. She blinked several times, then stammered, "I . . . I took it off. . . ."

Dr. Jordan turned to her. "Mirabel? You never take off that amulet. You call it your good-luck charm. I've never seen you without it."

"Of course I take it off sometimes," Ms. Cassatt replied. "Don't be ridiculous. We're getting off track here. Do I have to remind you, Malik, that if you'd been doing your job and watching these little thieves, we wouldn't be having this conversation? Luckily, I caught this one red-handed." Ms. Cassatt grabbed Cody's arm and pushed her over to Ms. Stad. "Take these brats out of here before I *do* call the police. You're lucky I don't press charges!"

Dr. Jordan turned to Ms. Cassatt. "Wait a minute, Mirabel. Let me see that Eye."

"What?" Ms. Cassatt said, clutching the amulet tightly in her hand.

"I said, let me see that," Dr. Jordan repeated.

"Why?" Ms. Cassatt said.

"I just want to make sure it's authentic."

Ms. Cassatt looked like a frightened cat trapped by a threatening dog. Her green eyes widened to the size of quarters. Slowly she opened her hand, revealing the artifact.

Dr. Jordan took it from her and flipped it over. Underneath were tiny carved hieroglyphs. But this Eye was different from the Eye the kids had first seen in the Life Studies room.

Code Buster's Key and Solution found on pp. 172, 177.

"Hmm," he muttered. He reached into his deep lab coat pocket, brought out his magnifying glasses, and put them on. After studying the small insignia, he withdrew a knife and scraped a small piece off the back. Then he removed his glasses and frowned. "There's real infiltration of the corrosion on the epidermis of the bronze metal, which cannot be faked."

Cody had no clue what he'd just said, other than the words "cannot be faked."

"This symbol," he continued, looking at the

inscription, "is the name of the god of hieroglyphs."
He steadied his gaze on Ms. Cassatt. "I'd still have to
do a few more tests, but I think this Eye of Horus is
authentic. Where's your necklace, Mirabel?"

Ms. Cassatt gave a nervous laugh. "I don't know.
The chain broke and I put it down somewhere. It's
only a replica. You know that."

"Check your pockets," Dr. Jordan said.

"What? I'm not going to—"

"You made Cody do it," Luke said. "Now you
should, too."

"There's nothing in my pockets," Ms. Cassatt said.
Her face had gone white.

"Yes, there is," M.E. said, pointing to the small
bulge in Ms. Cassatt's pants pocket.

Ms. Cassatt shook her head, then reached into her
pocket and withdrew a gold chain. But no pendant.

"It's the chain," Ms. Cassatt said, glaring at M.E.
"So what?"

"So where's the Eye that was hanging from it?"
Quinn asked.

"I told you a minute ago, I put it down somewhere

when the chain broke. You're not implying that—"

Dr. Jordan took the chain from Ms. Cassatt's hand and examined it. "There's nothing wrong with this chain."

"I'm telling you, it broke! I took the amulet off and set it down. I must have lost it. As I said, it was only a replica. It may have looked real, but I have a friend who makes excellent copies."

Dr. Jordan stared at Ms. Cassatt. "You know a forger?"

Ms. Cassatt grunted. "I wouldn't call him that. He's an artist."

"Most forgers are artists, Mirabel," Dr. Jordan said. He shook his head, as if disappointed in his colleague.

"Don't twist this around, Malik," Ms. Cassatt said. "I mean, maybe it was *you* who stole the Eye from the case and switched it with a fake. You have a key, just like me. And you know a lot about forgeries. Maybe *you* slipped the real one into that poor girl's pocket to make it look like she did it. Yes, maybe *you're* the thief, Malik Jordan."

"Well, let's call the police and have them settle this, then, shall we?" Dr. Jordan said.

But before he could get out his cell phone, Ms. Cassatt grabbed the amulet and ran from the room.

Chapter 9

L ock down!" Dr. Jordan called out as he ran after Ms. Cassatt. The kids and Ms. Stad followed him. Dr. Jordan grabbed the phone from the reception desk and repeated the urgent phrase through the intercom. His voice echoed throughout the museum.

Within seconds, two security guards arrived, keys jangling from their hands. The one with SIMON WOOD on his name tag ran to the front door and locked it, while the other one, DEBORAH WEINSTEIN, said, "Back doors are secure. What's happened?"

"Have you seen Mirabel?" Dr. Jordan asked them, his dark eyes darting around the room.

Both guards shook their heads.

"Search the museum. We have to find her!" he commanded. "She's stolen one of the artifacts."

The Code Busters and Ms. Stad stood frozen, watching the drama. Was Ms. Cassatt actually the thief? Where had she gone?

Dr. Jordan left the entry room and joined the guards in their search for the missing woman. Quinn turned to the others and finger-spelled:

Code Buster's Key and Solution found on pp. 171, 177.

Before Ms. Stad could stop them, the kids took off. They spread out, each one checking a different room, looking for any sign of Ms. Cassatt. Moments later, they met back in the lobby.

"No sign of her," M.E. said.

"Where could she have gone?" Cody asked.

"The lab?" Quinn suggested.

"Dr. Jordan and the guards went there," M.E. said.

"There's only one other place." Luke pointed to the dark tunnel that was blocked off by a sign that said NO ADMITTANCE. UNDER CONSTRUCTION.

The Code Busters looked at one another. The tunnel was supposed to resemble a hidden passageway like those in the ancient pyramids. Cody had been dying to see it.

The perfect place to hide, she thought.

The kids moved closer to explore the opening of the tunnel. It looked dark and kind of creepy. It reminded Cody of a mine entrance she'd seen in the California Gold Country, where she used to live. Above the entrance was a series of hieroglyphs. Cody pulled out her decoder card and quickly translated the message aloud.

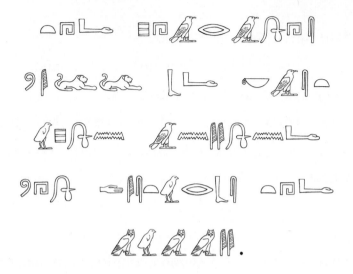

Code Buster's Key and Solution found on pp. 172, 177.

A chill crept up Cody's spine. While she didn't believe in things like curses, she still didn't like the message. She shrugged it off and stepped inside.

The opening was narrow—just tall and wide enough to allow one person to enter at a time. Cody felt a cold breeze on her arm, but looking ahead, she saw nothing except darkness.

"I'm going in," Cody said. She climbed over the rope that blocked the entrance and took a few steps into the chilly, dark tunnel.

She paused and listened.

Nothing.

Pulling out her cell phone, she tapped the flashlight app and shone it ahead. She took a few more steps, moving deeper into the tunnel, then stopped to listen for sounds.

She felt something touch her back and spun around.

"Luke!" she gasped. "You scared me! Don't creep up on me like that!"

"Sorry," Luke said. "Didn't want you to go in there alone."

Cody smiled. She turned toward the dark and shone her cell phone light into the deep recesses of the tunnel. The place totally creeped her out, especially when she thought about the mummy that lay in its tomb ahead.

She shivered.

There's no such thing as mummies coming back to life, she reminded herself a few times. But memories of scary movies featuring cloth-wrapped, zombified mummies were all she could think of. Thank goodness, Luke was right behind her. It was nice to have someone brave to back you up.

Suddenly, Cody heard a sound. A tapping, like Morse code. She turned to Luke. He was tapping on his cell phone, using the walkie-talkie app. She recognized the coded message he was sending to Quinn and M.E.

-. --- ... .. --. -. --- .

.-. -.-. .- ... .- - -

Code Buster's Key and Solution found on pp. 170, 177.

When Luke was done tapping, Cody continued deeper into the dimly lit darkness. She noticed that the tunnel began to widen, and glancing back, she could no longer see light coming from the tunnel entrance. She took another step, and another.

And then froze.

An eerie moan was coming from deeper inside. She grabbed Luke's arm. Her instinct was to run in the opposite direction and get out of this dark tunnel. But she told herself again, *Mummies aren't real. They don't moan. And they don't come back to life. Or try to kill you.*

Only real people did that.

Like Ms. Cassatt?

The moan came again, this time louder, creepier. It sounded as if someone was in pain.

Had Ms. Cassatt been injured? Had she fallen in the dark? Did she need help?

Cody was torn between wanting to run and wanting to see if Ms. Cassatt was hurt. Still holding Luke's arm, she took a few more steps through the twisting tunnel toward the sound.

When she stopped, she heard someone breathing heavily. It was coming from her right side. She flashed her cell phone light toward the noise, and screamed.

Ms. Cassatt stood tucked in a tiny alcove. Her eyes looked as wild as a feral cat's. In her hand she held a heavy-looking statue the size of a rolling pin.

She raised the object above her head, ready to bring it down on Cody's skull.

At the last second, Luke jerked Cody out of the way. She fell to the floor and scurried back on all fours.

"I'll get you, you little brats!" Ms. Cassatt screamed. She stepped out of the alcove and raised the object again.

"Stop!" came a voice from behind Cody. She turned to see Quinn and M.E. racing up the tunnel toward them. The light of Quinn's cell phone bounced as he ran.

"Stop!" Quinn screamed again. "You can't get all four of us, so you might as well put that down. Dr. Jordan is right behind us. He has the police with him."

Cody let out the breath she was holding. She was impressed at how forceful Quinn sounded—just like a cop on TV—but figured he was just as scared as she was.

Was he telling the truth about Dr. Jordan and the police? If they were right behind him, wouldn't she have heard them? Wouldn't they have arrived by now?

She had a sinking feeling Quinn was bluffing. But now what were they supposed to do?

Cody suddenly had an idea.

"Inn-quay, ou-yay istract-day er-hay ith-way obe-stray ight-lay app-ay," she said in pig Latin.

"What's all the gibberish?" Ms. Cassatt snapped, hoisting the weapon. "Knock it off or I'll knock your blocks off!" She started swinging the statue like a baseball bat.

Cody scrambled up and backed away. She saw Quinn tap his phone. What was taking him so long?

Finally, he held his phone toward Ms. Cassatt. Suddenly, a strobe light appeared, lighting up the dark tunnel with a blinding, pulsing light.

Ms. Cassatt covered her eyes.

"It's the police!" M.E. screamed. "They're here!"

Great trick, Cody thought. At least for the moment. Now there was only one thing left to do.

"Un-ray!" Cody yelled.

Code Buster's Solution found on pp. 177.

Chapter 10

The Code Busters darted through the twisting tunnel—smack into a large, dark figure. Cody shone her light on the man's face. A police officer! In the beam of her flashlight app, Cody saw two more uniformed cops behind him. Farther back, she caught a glimpse of Dr. Jordan.

"Whoa there! Slow down!" the officer said, holding up a hand. He shone his flashlight in Cody's face. "What's going on?"

Cody squinted at the bright light and pointed back into the tunnel. "She tried to kill me! My friends came . . ." Cody stopped to catch her breath.

"She's got a big, heavy statue," Quinn said.

"And she was about to hit Cody with it," Luke added.

"She's back there!" M.E. said, pointing into the darkness.

The officer directed his light into the black tunnel. "I don't see anything."

Dr. Jordan stepped forward. "Sergeant Casey, if the kids say Mirabel Cassatt is back there, then she is. I'd consider her desperate and dangerous."

"Okay, everyone, stand back," Sergeant Casey said to the group. He turned to another officer. "Finsilver, stay here with these people. Parker, follow me. Let's go."

Officer Finsilver began herding the kids and Dr. Jordan back toward the entrance, his flashlight illuminating the way. Sergeant Casey and Officer Parker continued down the dark hallway. The sergeant's flashlight beam bounced off the tunnel walls. Moments later, they were out of sight.

Suddenly, Cody heard a *boom*! She jumped. M.E. grabbed Cody's arm in fear.

"Keep away from me!" Cody heard Ms. Cassatt's loud voice echo from the depths of the model tomb. "I'll smash this mummy to pieces. Then this stupid museum won't be so special anymore."

Dr. Jordan ran forward, past Officer Finsilver and the Code Busters, a look of terror on his eerily lit face.

"Mirabel! No! Please! You know how much the museum relies on that mummy for visitor traffic. It's irreplaceable. Please, just come out. Let's talk about this."

Officer Finsilver began following Dr. Jordan, calling, "Sir! Come back! Sir!"

The Code Busters were right behind him.

"Ha!" Cody heard Ms. Cassatt's hollow voice bounce off the walls of the tunnel. "You can't fool me, Malik. The minute I do that, the cops will arrest me. No, we're going to do this my way."

The officer caught up with Dr. Jordan and grabbed

his arm, trying to stop him. Dr. Jordan shook it off. "We have to stop her!" he said. "We can't afford to lose our mummy. It's our biggest draw."

"Back up!" Officer Finsilver ordered.

Sergeant Casey's voice rang out again. "What do you want, Ms. Cassatt? Let's end this thing peacefully."

"I want you to send in one of the kids so I can protect myself and get out of here safely," she called back. "I want the rest of you to back out of the tunnel and leave the museum!"

Cody felt a chill run through her. Ms. Cassatt wanted one of the Code Busters?

"Not going to happen, Ms. Cassatt," the sergeant said. "We're not putting any of these kids at risk, and you know it. You can just forget about—"

Before Sergeant Casey could finish his words, Cody turned to M.E. She had a plan. Cody tapped out a message in Morse Code on her friend's arm:

-   .   .-..   .-..

.-..   ..-   -.-   .   .-   -.   -..

--.-　　..-　　..　　-.　　-.　　-　　---

--　　.　　.　　-　　..　　-.

-...　　.-　　-　　....　　.-.　　---　　---　　--

Code Buster's Key and Solution found on pp. 170, 177.

As soon as Cody's message spread via arm taps to the other Code Busters, the four kids quietly backed down the tunnel, leaving behind Dr. Jordan and the officer. Cody heard the sergeant continue trying to negotiate with Ms. Cassatt, his voice fading as the friends made their way to the entrance. Cody hoped they would keep arguing so the Code Busters would have time to put her plan into action.

"Are you kids okay?" Ms. Stad asked when she saw them exit the tunnel. She rushed up and hugged all four of them at once.

"We're fine," Cody said. "We . . . uh, I have to go to the bathroom."

"Me too," said Quinn.

"Well, hurry back!" Ms. Stad called. "I'm taking you out of here immediately! Mr. Pike and the other students are waiting for us on the bus."

Luke shook his head. "We can't leave. They locked us in, remember."

"Then you're not leaving my sight," Ms. Stad said.

The kids headed for the restrooms at the far side of the lobby.

"Quinn and I can't go in there!" Luke whispered to Cody after she started inside the girls' bathroom. "We'll get arrested, or something."

"No, you won't!" Cody said. "Don't be such a chicken. It's just a bathroom." Cody was surprised that such a brave kid was afraid of the girls' room. Of course, she'd probably feel the same way if she had to go into the boys' bathroom.

Quinn looked at Luke and shrugged, then followed Cody and M.E. inside. After Luke looked around to see if anyone was watching, he entered the small room.

"What are we doing in here?" Luke whispered nervously.

Instead of answering him, Cody said, "I saw extra rolls of toilet paper on the backs of the toilets. Quick, grab a bunch."

They did as Cody directed, then returned, each carrying a few rolls.

"Now what?" asked M.E.

"Now let's make a mummy!" Cody said, grinning. She looked at Luke. "You're the tallest, so you're going to be the mummy. Come on, let's start wrapping! And hurry! We don't have much time."

Luke grimaced, but stood still as the others began to wrap his arms, legs, torso, and head with toilet paper.

"Don't cover his eyes," Cody told Quinn, who was wrapping Luke's face with multiple layers. "He has to be able to see."

With the three of them working together, the kids managed to turn Luke into a pretty cool-looking mummy in only a few minutes. Cody stood back and admired their work. She tucked in several loose ends, then said to Luke, "Perfect! Can you walk?"

Luke raised his arms like a zombie and took a few stiff steps forward. *He even walks like a mummy,* Cody thought. *This just might work.*

"Quinn, give me your phone," she said.

"Why? You have your own phone."

"I'll be using mine, and Luke needs one."

Quinn handed his cell phone to Cody. She quickly searched the apps site, then loaded a new app.

"Okay, come on. We have to get back before it's too late." Cody explained the details of her plan as they headed for the tunnel. When they neared the entrance, she saw Dr. Jordan, Officer Finsilver, and Ms. Stad standing just outside the opening.

Ms. Stad turned around. "What took you so—" she began to say. She stopped when her eyes fell on Luke the Mummy. She gasped. "What in the world are you kids . . ."

Cody looked at the others, then finger-spelled,

☞👌 !

Code Buster's Key and Solution found on pp. 171, 177.

Without saying a word, the kids ran into the dark tunnel, their path lit only by Cody's cell phone light.

"Hey, stop!" Officer Finsilver yelled. He started after them, but they were faster than the cop, who was laden with heavy police gear. He wasn't quite as nimble in taking the twists and turns of the tunnel. Moments later, the Code Busters spotted Sergeant Casey, his back to them.

Beyond him, in the beam of the sergeant's flashlight, Cody saw the shadowed form of Ms. Cassatt. She stood holding the heavy statue, her thickly outlined eyes wild with desperation.

Cody turned to Luke. "Get down before she sees you," she whispered to the mummy. He ducked down, then knelt on his hands and knees.

Sergeant Casey whirled around when he heard Cody. "What are you kids doing here? Get back! Where's Officer Finsilver?"

Officer Finsilver arrived seconds later, huffing and puffing. "They were too fast!" he cried. "I couldn't stop them!"

Ignoring the sergeant, Cody raised her arms and called out, "Ms. Cassatt? It's me, Cody. You said you wanted a kid so you could get out of here? I'm the one who got us into this mess, so I'm volunteering."

Sergeant Casey stared at her. "Oh no you're not! Not on my watch!"

"Smart move, girl!" Ms. Cassatt called out. "Now, hurry up. The rest of you, get out now! Or the mummy gets it."

Cody turned and whispered her plan to the sergeant. He shook his head. "No way. Too dangerous," he said.

She looked at Ms. Cassatt, who was standing about five feet away, her face drawn, eyes menacing. Between the sergeant and Ms. Cassatt sat a decorative sarcophagus large enough to hold a human body. The Plexiglas top lay open and had been pushed aside. Cody nodded to Luke. He took his cue and began crawling toward the front of the sarcophagus, keeping low to remain hidden by the massive artifact.

"Back off!" Ms. Cassatt yelled at the sergeant again. "I mean it. Once I'm out of here, you can have the kid back. Until then, she's my insurance policy. Clear the tunnel!"

Cody whispered to the sergeant, "Shine the light right in her face."

The sergeant frowned but then did as she asked.

Ms. Cassatt immediately turned away from the blinding light. As she did, Luke stretched out on the floor on the sergeant's side of the tomb.

Meanwhile, Cody slipped her phone out of her pocket and prepared to press an app icon.

"Come here, you little brat!" Ms. Cassatt commanded Cody. "The rest of you, beat it!" She held the heavy statue over her head, ready to bring it down on the priceless mummy inside the open tomb.

Cody pressed the icon on her phone. A red light filled the dark room and began to pulsate.

"Miiiiirraaaaabbbbeeelllll Caaassssaaattttt . . . ," echoed a low, unearthly voice.

Nice job, Luke, Cody thought. She swore he sounded just like a mummy speaking from the dead for the first time in centuries.

A claw-shaped hand, wrapped in layers of white toilet paper, suddenly shot up from behind the sarcophagus, casting a giant shadow on the walls from the flashlight beam.

Then an arm appeared . . .

And a shoulder . . .

And a head . . .

A body rose up, its arms extended, eerily facing Ms. Cassatt.

The hideous voice came again: "Miiiiiirrrrr-aaaaaabeelllllllll Caaaaaaaaasssssssaaatttt . . ."

Luke the Mummy leaned toward the frightened woman, his clawed hands reaching for her.

Ms. Cassatt gave a deafening scream and dropped the statue.

Chapter 11

"N ice going!" Sergeant Casey said to the Code Busters, after he and his two officers had taken Ms. Cassatt into custody. "You kids took a very big risk, and you could have gotten seriously hurt, but it was clever of you to dress like a mummy, son, and make all those weird sounds."

Now that the standoff was over, the kids were back in the museum lobby, talking to the sergeant and Dr. Jordan. Ms. Stad had a protective arm wrapped around M.E. and was listening as the Code Busters explained the details of their plan.

"We figured if we distracted Ms. Cassatt, you might have a chance to get her," Cody said to the sergeant.

He shook his head. "Yeah, but it could have backfired, you know."

The kids nodded.

"How did you make your voice sound like a mummy's?" Dr. Jordan asked.

Quinn explained, "There's an app for that. It's called Scary Voice Changer. You can do all kinds of things with your voice—sound like a robot or a mouse or an alien. Or make it sound like you're underwater. You can even add an echo."

"The mummy app is awesome," Luke said, grinning. He had pulled most of the toilet paper off, but a few pieces were still stuck inside his waistband and in his shoes. "Oooawwwww," he added, demonstrating the mummy sound while wiggling his fingers.

"How did you know she was afraid of mummies?" Ms. Stad asked. She gave M.E. a squeeze.

"We didn't," M.E. answered. "But we figured,

after she'd spent all these years hanging out with mummies, we might at least startle her."

"Well, you did that," the sergeant said. "I especially liked the flashing red light. I suppose you used an app for that, too?"

Cody nodded, then touched the icon on her phone. The room lit up with swirling red light.

"Pretty cool," Dr. Jordan said. "I might have to add those tricks when I give talks to students. Maybe I'll even dress up like a mummy and use that mummy voice."

Ms. Stad arched her eyebrow.

"Then again, maybe not," he said, grinning sheepishly.

"So, what's going to happen to Ms. Cassatt?" Quinn asked.

"For now, jail," the sergeant said. "I've got a couple of officers checking out her home. I have a feeling we'll find more artifacts she might have 'replaced.'"

"Is she a real forger?" Luke asked.

Dr. Jordan shook his head. "I doubt it. That's quite a skill to master. But she knows a lot of people in the world of artifacts—some reputable, some not. It wouldn't be difficult for her to find a forger to make the fakes."

"Then all she'd have to do is switch the real ones with the replicas when no one was around," Quinn said. "I saw that in a movie once."

"Yeah," Luke said. "Then she could sell them on the black market."

"Or keep them for herself," M.E. added, "and pretend they were reproductions. I wouldn't mind having some fake Egyptian jewelry to wear."

"Can you get those things back from the black market?" Quinn asked.

"Sometimes they turn up," Dr. Jordan said. "But often they go missing for decades. It's a good thing you figured out what she was doing; otherwise, it could have been a lot worse."

"Why did she do it?" Cody asked, shaking her head.

"Who knows why some people become greedy?" Dr. Jordan answered, holding up the recovered Eye of Horus and admiring it. "It's not always easy being around all these beautiful treasures, knowing you'll never own them. Mirabel Cassatt loved her jewelry. I suppose she got tired of wearing imitations and wanted the real thing. And working here, she thought she could get away with it."

"But she tried to make it look like I stole that Eye of Horus!" Cody said.

Dr. Jordan nodded. "She must have dropped it in your pocket at some point, to take the focus off herself."

Cody remembered when Ms. Cassatt bumped into her, just before she accused her of stealing the artifact. That would have been the perfect opportunity to slip the Eye into her pocket. Sort of like a pickpocket, but in reverse.

"Well, I'm just glad this is over," Ms. Stad said. "We're going to be very late getting all the students back to school. Our volunteers are calling the parents so they won't worry. I just hope we'll still be allowed to go on more field trips."

"Me too," said Quinn. "'Cause this one was awesome!" He fist-bumped Luke.

The adults laughed and shook their heads.

Awesome? Cody thought about the close call she'd had with Ms. Cassatt and shivered. If it hadn't been for her friends, she might have ended up sharing eternal space with that old mummy. Not so awesome. But it was still nice to know she had helped save a bit of priceless history today.

While the adults chatted, Cody turned to her friends and signed,

Code Buster's Key and Solution found on pp. 171, 178.

Then they all linked their index fingers—Cody to Luke, Luke to M.E., M.E. to Quinn, and Quinn back to Cody—to form a circle. It was the American Sign Language sign for "friendship."

Chapter 12

The Code Busters, along with the other sixth graders, were tired when they arrived back at school. It was an hour past the last bell, and the rest of the student body had gone home. Luckily, the kids had the weekend to rest up before school on Monday.

After a good night's sleep, Cody and her friends spent most of Saturday in their clubhouse, reliving the adventure.

"That field trip was awesome," Quinn said as he sat down on the carpeted floor.

Luke nodded. "Dude, we actually discovered a forgery. How cool is that?"

"Pretty amazing," Cody said, "even though it almost got us in trouble."

"Yeah," M.E. added. "I'm surprised Matt the Brat didn't have anything to do with it."

The kids laughed. *That is a first*, Cody thought. He was the one who usually caused trouble. Maybe he was getting better. Cody shook her head. Naw, not Matt the Brat.

M.E. looked at Cody. "Why did you shake your head just now?"

Cody smiled. "No reason. Just thinking about everything. You know, we never did figure out who drew that last picture in the classroom. Or what it meant."

"I guess we'll have to wait until Monday for the answer," Luke said.

"Yeah, but what if Stad doesn't know either?" Quinn added. "And what if the person who did it never confesses?"

Cody nodded thoughtfully. "Steganography is

what started all of this—and that assignment to draw those pictures with hidden messages inside."

"In a way, steganography is what led us to discover the fake Eye of Horus," Luke said. "The Eye was hidden right in front of our eyes. We just didn't see it at first."

"Well, I love learning Egyptian hieroglyphs," M.E. said. "It's weird that people first thought they were just drawings of birds and hooks and things, but after that guy cracked the code, those symbols turned out to be letters and words."

"Yeah, hieroglyphs are cool," Cody said, sketching the Eye of Horus in her Code Busters notebook. "We need to use them more when we send secret messages. And steganography, too."

"Except that everyone in class has a decoder card for hieroglyphs, so our messages won't be very secret," M.E. said, staring at Cody's drawing. Cody used a ruler as she sketched each part of the Eye. When she was done, she labeled the sections with fractions.

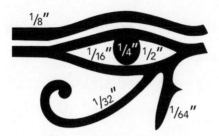

"What's that for?" M.E. asked.

"Nothing special," Cody said. "I just think it's cool how you can use the Eye to measure stuff if you don't have a ruler," Cody said. "Each part measures part of an inch—one-half, one-fourth, one-eighth. Even measurements were hidden in the Eye."

"That Eye of Horus is full of mystery," M.E. said. "And so was Ms. Cassatt."

"Dude, I'm glad we figured out what she was doing with that Eye," Luke said. "Otherwise, the fake one might never have been discovered."

"Did Ms. Cassatt really think she wouldn't get caught?" M.E. asked.

"Seriously!" Luke said. "She even wore the fake in plain sight. Still, she fooled a lot of people."

"Well," Quinn said, "we learned other ways to send secret messages, too, like knitting Morse code with yarn and writing sentences with *i*'s and *t*'s for dots and dashes."

"Or shaving your head and tattooing a message," Luke added, then he readjusted his Saints cap. "Dude, no way am I shaving my head just to send a code."

Cody laughed.

"And we learned about hidden symbols on money," Quinn said. He took out a five-dollar bill and held it up to the light. "There's the watermark and the security thread. I guess this one isn't counterfeit."

The kids smiled.

"My favorite code is still hieroglyphs," Cody said. "There are so many ways you can use them to send messages. Maybe we should invent our own style of glyphs."

"Great idea," M.E. said. "Like, the letter *a* could be a drawing of an apple or an airplane. *B* could be a ball or a bat. *C* could be a cat or a crown."

"Sure," Cody said, "those are all pretty easy to draw. Or we could just use symbols from the computer. That way, we could send secret computer messages."

Quinn got out his Code Busters notebook and a pencil. "Let's get to work. We've got some Code Buster glyphs to create!"

When the four kids returned to school on Monday, they had completed their own glyph code using computer keyboard symbols and had e-mailed each other secret messages.

M.E. had written:

- □ ! ∞ ● ! ^ ! = % % ☼ %
♪ ^ * ♪ △ ≠ √

Luke had sent:

- ? - = % $ @ % - ∞ & !
X ≠ X X ☼

Quinn had typed:

? % ● √ @ ≠ - ? $! ↑ ☼ △ ! x - $

And Cody had e-mailed:

↑ ≠ ∞ = - ∞ - √ ! ∞

% & ☼ ↑ ● - ! ∞   # ! ●

Code Buster's Key and Solution found on pp. 172, 178.

They'd also printed out some coded messages and hidden them in their secret hiding places. Cody found a note in the knothole of the ash tree in her yard. M.E.'s message was tucked inside her flower box. Luke's was under the doorstep of his *grand-mère*'s condo. And Quinn spotted his in the family doghouse. Cody was totally hooked on creating her own glyphs and couldn't wait to do more.

When they reached Berkeley Cooperative Middle School, Cody and M.E. waved good-bye to Luke and Quinn, and the pairs headed for their own class-rooms. When the girls entered Ms. Stad's room, they noticed the last drawing was still taped to the white-board.

It looked to Cody like the hidden picture still hadn't been solved.

"Good morning, class!" Ms. Stad greeted the students after they were settled at their desks. "I hope you had a good time at the museum—in spite of all the drama. As you know, two of our students, along with two students from Mr. Pike's class, did a little 'extra credit' work while they were there." She paused and smiled at Cody and M.E. "Thanks to their keen eyes and what they learned about fakes and forgeries, they were able to catch a thief in the act of stealing a valuable artifact and save the Egyptian Museum a lot of money. How about a round of applause for Cody and M.E.!"

The kids clapped—all except for Matt the Brat, who turned and gave Cody the stink-eye. Cody ignored him, figuring he was just jealous about the attention she and M.E. were getting.

"And now I have a surprise," Ms. Stad continued. "We have a special guest today." She opened the classroom door and in walked Dr. Jordan. The kids clapped, happy to see the museum art expert.

"Hi, students!" Dr. Jordan said, greeting the group of sixth graders. He turned to the teacher. "Thanks for the invitation to come and visit your classroom, Ms. Stadelhofer."

"We're so happy to see you again, Dr. Jordan. Welcome." She turned back to her students. "Dr. Jordan is here to help us solve a mystery."

The class grew quiet in anticipation. Cody wondered what mystery Dr. Jordan could solve in their ordinary classroom. It certainly wasn't like the museum, which was full of mysteries, puzzles, codes, and riddles.

"Dr. Jordan, we're stumped," Ms. Stad said to him. "Last week, I asked the students to create their own hidden pictures."

Dr. Jordan nodded. "Ah, yes. Steganography. How did they do?"

"Excellently!" Ms. Stad said. "They solved all of the picture puzzles—except one." She pointed to the lone picture on the whiteboard and the Egyptian hieroglyphs underneath. "We wondered if you could help us, since you're an expert in Egyptian art and hieroglyphic writing."

Code Buster's Key and Solution found on pp. 172, 178.

Dr. Jordan studied the drawing of an eye inside a triangle and the hieroglyphs below.

"The students used their hieroglyphic decoder cards to translate the symbols," Ms. Stad continued, "but the letters made no sense. Maybe you can help us crack the code?"

Dr. Jordan nodded. "That's the Eye of Providence that watches over all of us. You'll find the symbol on the one-dollar bill." Dr. Jordan focused on the hieroglyphs. Then he drew in a deep breath, let it out, and said, "Aha!"

"You've figured out the message?" Ms. Stad said, her eyebrows raised in excitement. Cody wondered if Ms. Stad really knew the answer already.

"I think I have," Dr. Jordan said. "But before I tell you, I'll give you all a clue. Write out the message on a piece of paper in the same pattern as the hieroglyphs."

Cody and the rest of the students pulled out pencil, paper, and their hieroglyphic decoder cards, and wrote down the translation, using the same pattern that was on the paper. The message formed three rows of seven letters. Cody tried to make sense of the letters, but she didn't recognize any words. They were just nonsense.

W O I W A G T !
E G N O S N O C
R E G T H I N D

When the students were done, Dr. Jordan asked, "Do any of you see the message yet?"

The kids shook their heads no.

"All right, here's another hint. The hieroglyphic script is very flexible. It can be read from left to right, right to left, or *up and down*."

M.E. raised her hand. "How do we know which direction to read it?"

Dr. Jordan smiled mysteriously. "Good question! To figure out how to read the text, you need to notice which way the animals or people glyphs are facing. They always look toward the beginning of the text."

A collective "ooh" came from the students. Pencils busily moved into action as the kids took another stab at the translation. Cody studied the symbols carefully, and finally noticed the trick. She began reading the translation, first moving down the column, then up, and so on. Moments later, she had cracked the coded message!

"Seriously?" Cody squealed as soon as she knew the answer. Ms. Stad winked at her. She had known what the message said all along! Moments later, Cody heard the rest of the students gasping, giggling, and slapping high fives.

"It sounds like you've figured out the message,"

Ms. Stad said. "It's true—we're going on a trip to Washington, DC, to visit the Smithsonian museums, experience the Cherry Blossom Festival, and check out the International Spy Museum."

The students yelled "Yippee!" "Awesome!" "Cool!" and "Sweet!"

Cody raised her hand. "Ms. Stadelhofer, did you draw that message?"

Ms. Stad nodded. "Ah, you figured that out. Well, I have another surprise for you." She turned to their guest. "Dr. Jordan?"

He glanced around at the students, then finally he began, "I was trying to think of a way to say thanks to the kids who helped catch the thief. I'm happy to say, the Egyptian Museum is paying for your tickets to DC."

More whoops, hollers, and high fives. The students were ecstatic. Cody couldn't believe it. A free trip to the nation's capital! And who knew? Maybe they'd even discover some secret codes while they were there—especially at the Spy Museum. She couldn't wait for the trip to begin!

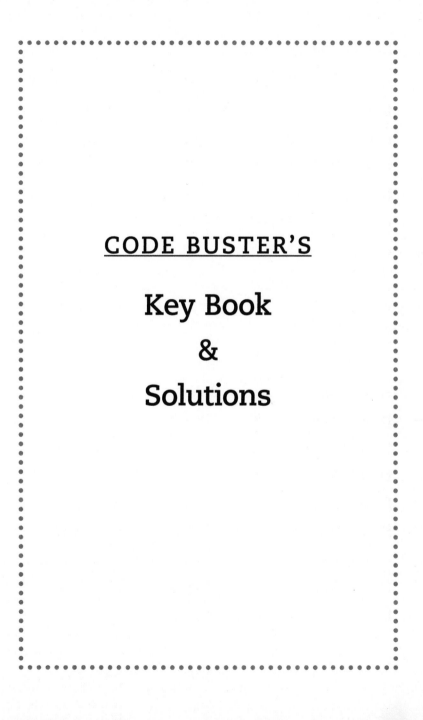

CODE BUSTER'S

Key Book
&
Solutions

Morse Code:

A .-	**H**	**O** ---	**V** ...-
B -...	**I** ..	**P** .--.	**W** .--
C -.-.	**J** .---	**Q** --.-	**X** -..-
D -..	**K** -.-	**R** .-.	**Y** -.--
E .	**L** .-..	**S** ...	**Z** --..
F ..-.	**M** --	**T** -	
G --.	**N** -.	**U** ..-	

Phonetic Alphabet:

A = Alphabet	J = Juliet	S = Sierra
B = Bravo	K = Kilo	T = Tango
C = Charlie	L = Lima	U = Uniform
D = Delta	M = Mike	V = Victor
E = Echo	N = November	W = Whiskey
F = Foxtrot	O = Oscar	X = X-ray
G = Golf	P = Papa	Y = Yankee
H = Hotel	Q = Quebec	Z = Zulu
I = India	R = Romeo	

Semaphore Code:

Finger Spelling:

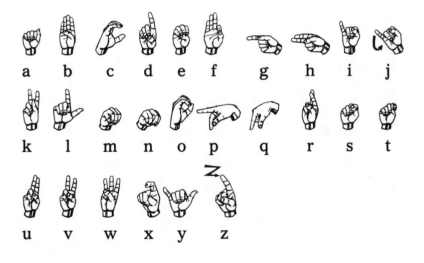

Egyptian Hieroglyphics:

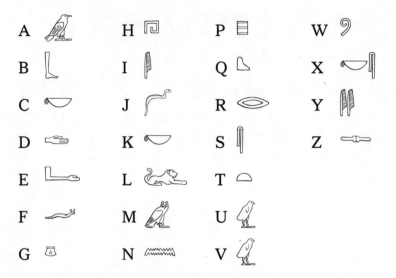

Code Busters' Glyph Code:

!	@	#	$	%	^	&	*
A	B	C	D	E	F	G	H
-	+	=	?	X	∞	♪	↑
I	J	K	L	M	N	O	P
Δ	△	√	●	≠	♥	□	☺
Q	R	S	T	U	V	W	X
☼	◊						
Y	Z						

Chapter 1

Finger spelling: **Hieroglyphs**

Egyptian hieroglyphics: **Steganography**

Finger spelling: **Yarn code. Cool.**

Drawings code: **Hidden**

Photo code: **Code**

Chapter 2

Hidden word puzzle: **Can you read me**

c

l**a**y

li**n**es

red**y**arn

artc**o**lors

huegl**u**eblue

purple**r**ibbons

pinkgre**e**nlights

ayellowp**a**intbrush

artcanvas**d**esigndark

i**m**e

s**e**e

Maze puzzle: **You can hide a whole sentence as long as you follow the words**

Hidden letter code: **spy**

Hidden Morse code: **Code Busters**

t i t i	t t t	t i i	i
- . - .	- - -	- . .	.
c	o	d	e

Semaphore code: **busters**

<u>Chapter 3</u>

Morse code: **DJ, ME**

Backward code: **Monday**

Egyptian hieroglyphics:

I want to see the mummies!

I love Egyptian jewelery!

Maybe they have a Rosetta Stone.

I'm hungry! Are we there yet?

Egyptian hieroglyphics: **Sphinx**

Chapter 4

Anagrams:

1. **Isis**
2. **Amun**
3. **Anubis**
4. **Bastet**
5. **Horus**
6. **Maat**
7. **Osiris**
8. **Sekhmet**
9. **Sobek**
10. **Thoth**

Egyptian hieroglyphics: **Eye of Horus**

Chapter 5

Egyptian hieroglyphics: **An Eye for an I**

Egyptian hieroglyphics:

1. **What is a mummy's favorite type of music?** *Rap music.*
2. **What do you call a skeleton that lies in its grave?** *Lazy bones.*

3. **What do you get when you put a bow on a mummy?** *A wrapped present.*
4. **Why couldn't the mummy cross the road?** *He didn't have any guts.*
5. **Why was the little ghoul crying?** *Because he lost his mummy.*
6. **What do you call a mummy eating crackers in bed?** *A crummy mummy.*
7. **Why don't mummies play music in church?** *They have no organs.*
8. **Where do you go when a mummy is chasing you?** *To the living room.*
9. **Why don't mummies take vacations?** *They don't like to unwind.*

Chapter 6

Morse code: **Meet me in workroom. CodeRed.**

Finger spelling:

We can't leave. We have to search the museum!

Tell the others!

What? Why?

Semaphore code: **Run**

Chapter 7

Phonetic alphabet code: **Cassatt!**

Chapter 8

Morse code: **She tricked you**

Morse code: **Necklace**

Egyptian hieroglyphics: **Thoth**

Chapter 9

Finger spelling: **Let's go help find her!**

Egyptian hieroglyphics: **The Curse of the Pharaohs will be cast upon anyone who disturbs the mummy.**

Morse code: **No sign of Cassat**

Pig Latin: **Quinn, you distract her with strobe light app. Run!**

Chapter 10

Morse code: **Tell Luke and Quinn to meet in bathroom**

Finger spelling: **Go!**

Chapter 11
Finger spelling: **Code Busters rule!**

Chapter 12
Code Busters' glyph code:
I want a fake Eye of Horus
I liked being a mummy
Let's build a pyramid
Punkin is an Egyptian cat
Egyptian hieroglyphics:
We're going to Washington, DC!

Finger Spelling:
Chapter Title Translations
Chapter 1 *Eye Spy*
Chapter 2 *A Puzzle within a Puzzle*
Chapter 3 *Thirteen Secrets*
Chapter 4 *Fakes and Forgeries*
Chapter 5 *An Eye for an I*
Chapter 6 *Thirteen*
Chapter 7 *Time Is Running Out!*

Suggestions for How Teachers Can Use the Code Busters Club Series in the Classroom

Kids love codes. They will want to "solve" the codes in this novel before looking up the solutions. This means they will be practicing skills that are necessary to their class work in several courses, but in a non-pressured way.

The codes in this book vary in level of difficulty, so there is something for students of every ability. The codes move from a simple substitution of words for letters—a phonetic alphabet code—to more widely accepted "code" languages such as Morse code and semaphore.

In a mathematics classroom, the codes in this book can easily be used as motivational devices to teach problem solving and reasoning skills. Both of these have become important elements in the curriculum at all grade levels. The emphasis throughout the book on regarding codes as *patterns* gives students a great deal of practice in one of the primary strategies of problem solving. The strategy of "Looking for a Pattern" is basic to much of mathematics. The resolving of codes demonstrates how important patterns are. These codes can lead to discussions of the logic behind why they "work" (problem solving). The teacher can then have the students create their own codes (problem formulation) and try sending secret messages to one another, while other students try to "break the code." Developing and resolving these new codes will require a great deal of careful reasoning on the part of the students. The class might also wish to do some practical research in statistics, to determine which letters occur most frequently in the English language. (*E, T, A, O,* and *N* are the five most widely used letters, and should appear most often in coded messages.)

This book may also be used in other classroom areas of study, such as social studies, with its references to Ancient Egypt and codes employed during wartime. This book raises questions such as "Why would semaphore be important today? Where is it still used?"

In the English classroom, spelling is approached as a "deciphering code." The teacher may also suggest the students do some outside reading. They might read a biography of Samuel Morse or Louis Braille, or even the Sherlock Holmes mystery "The Adventure of the Dancing Men."

This book also refers to modern texting on cell phones and computers as a form of code. Students could explain what the various "code" abbreviations they use mean today and why they are used.   —*Dr. Stephen Krulik*

Dr. Stephen Krulik has a distinguished career as a professor of mathematics education. Professor emeritus at Temple University, he received the 2011 Lifetime Achievement Award from the National Council of Teachers of Mathematics.

ACKNOWLEDGMENTS

Thanks to Regina Griffin, Alison Weiss, Margaret Coffee, Michelle Bayuk, Katie Halata, Stefanie Von Borstal, Sara Sciuto, and Lily Ghahremani for all their expertise and assistance.

Thanks to Colleen Casey, Janet Finsilver, Staci McLaughlin, Ann Parker, and Carole Price for their insight and support.

And thanks to all the Code Busters Club members and fans for cracking all the codes!